IMMINENT THREAT

BY KIMBERLY ROSE JOHNSON

Imminent Threat
Published by Sweet Rose Press LLC
U.S.A.

This is a work of fiction. Names, characters, places and incidents are either the product of the author's imagination or are used fictitiously, and any resemblance to actual persons, living or dead, business establishments, events or locales is entirely coincidental.

All Scripture quotations, unless otherwise indicated, are taken from the Holy Bible, New International Version®, NIV®. Copyright ©1973, 1978, 1984, 2011 by Biblica, Inc.™ Used by permission of Zondervan. All rights reserved worldwide. www.zondervan.com The "NIV" and "New International Version" are trademarks registered in the United States Patent and Trademark Office by Biblica, Inc.™

ISBN 978-0-9984315-8-1

1

Jenna Walsh jerked back from her computer. A horrifying message in blood red flashed on the screen with the picture of a woman floating face down in a body of water.

This could be you.

Her heart raced as she rushed to her boss's office. She barged in without knocking. "Josh, I received a disturbing e-mail. As in we need to notify the authorities."

He looked up at her, wearing a frown. "Come in and close the door. I was going to send for you. We need to talk."

"Did you hear what I said? Someone sent me what looks like a death threat." Saying the words made Jenna's stomach roil.

He pointed to a vacant chair. "We have a bigger issue to discuss."

"Bigger than a threat on my life?" Her entire body shook. Jenna sank onto the leather chair, glancing toward the door as she did. She was safe in Josh's office, wasn't she? "What's this about? I presume not the e-mail I just received."

"Correct. Are you aware a video was recorded of you ranting about Kratt Paper?" Eyes of steel held her gaze.

"The paper company that hated my pitch?"

He nodded. "One and the same. It's gone viral."

"What are you talking about?" This was the first she'd heard of any video.

"Google yourself."

She pulled out her phone and did as he suggested. She clicked on a video of her face and gasped. "How did this get online?"

"More importantly, why would you say such things about our biggest client? Not only that, you're clearly in the Ads by Design office while disparaging our biggest client." His voice rose with every word.

Jenna scrolled down to see the comments and caught her breath. Everyone hated her. No one cared that a huge paper company with unethical practices was polluting the Puget Sound. They only trashed her.

"Are you listening to me?" Josh snapped.

She dragged her focus from her phone and met his livid gaze. "I was e-mailed a death theat."

"So you said. Now you know why."

Her head jerked as if slapped. "Are you suggesting someone threatened me because of that video?"

"How should I know?" He made eye contact with

her. "I have to do damage control. It's not personal. I understand getting angry, but Jenna you really need to think before you speak."

A sinking feeling washed over her.

"You've done an excellent job while you've been with us, but you're done here effective immediately. After that video, I suspect you're finished in the ad business. No one will want you on their team now. You have twenty minutes to clean out your desk and vacate the building. You're banished indefinitely from the premises. Security has your picture, so don't forget anything because they won't let you in."

Jenna's face heated. "Someone wants me dead, and you're firing me?" This couldn't be happening.

His face softened. "It gets worse. You must vacate the condo immediately. Leave the company car keys on the kitchen counter."

"But where will I go?" Her executive suite and car had been perks of the job. She was their top ad designer and brought in the clientele that more than supported the company's extravagance.

"Don't your parents live in Seattle?"

"Yes, but I can't go home." They would be so ashamed of her. She would never hear the end of it.

"Beats the alternative." He tapped his watch. "Better get a move on. You've already wasted two minutes."

She stood with clenched fists. Her throat thickened and the backs of her eyes burned as she left his office in a daze. She bumped into someone with a head of chestnut brown hair. She blew out a breath as she focused on the woman. "Samantha, you won't believe what happened."

Samantha Greene's eyes held pity. "You were fired. I heard. The entire office knows."

"How? I just found out?"

"Loose lips." She motioned toward Josh's assistant. "Where are you going to stay?"

Jenna was homeless, and going to her parents' place was out of the question—the humiliation was too much. The weight of the consequences of her actions overwhelmed her. She couldn't find her voice.

Samantha rested a hand on Jenna's forearm. "How about you come stay with me? You can sleep on my couch and figure out your next step."

"Really. You'd do that for me?"

"Yes, but don't tell anyone." She looked over her shoulder and lowered her voice. "I don't want the vultures to turn on me too."

Jenna nodded. "I need to get my stuff and leave. I'll call you later. Thanks." She hustled to her desk. "Polly, I'm glad you're here."

Her assistant looked up from her computer. She'd started as a summer intern and had earned her place as Jenna's personal assistant. What would happen to her now?

"Is there something I can do for you?" She blinked her hazel green eyes and brushed her hair behind her ears.

"I imagine you've heard the news?"

Polly sucked in her bottom lip and nodded. "I'm sorry. I know you'll land on your feet."

"Thanks. I'm sure Josh will let you stay on. You've proven yourself to be a valuable asset, so don't worry. Whoever replaces me will need an assistant." Jenna wiggled the mouse to wake up her computer screen. "You haven't received any odd calls for me or any suspicious mail, have you?"

"No. Why?"

"It's nothing." Maybe the e-mail was a bad joke or a warning from someone about her impending firing. She sucked in a breath. That had to be what it was—someone's cruel idea of a joke. Relief poured through her, but just the same, she forwarded the threat to her personal account. Maybe she could figure out who sent it.

Ten minutes later, her meager belongings were packed in a small box, and she left the building.

Her heels clicked on the downtown Seattle sidewalk. She glanced over her shoulder repeatedly as she moved toward the parking garage a block away. The threat on the computer haunted her, cruel joke or not. A car backfired. She screamed.

A man and a woman looked at her as if she was crazy and kept walking.

A horn blared, engines roared, bus brakes squealed—Jenna glanced around for anyone who appeared not to belong. Was the person who sent the death threat following her right now, or had it really only been a sick joke from one of her colleagues, rather former colleagues? She picked up her pace, desperate to get to the safety of her car. Or at least what once was her car. What was she going to do?

One Week Later

Jenna's finger hovered over the green button on her phone. There was no going back if she pressed it. "I can't do it, Samantha. There's no point." She tossed the phone onto her friend's sofa—her temporary bed.

Samantha Greene crossed her arms. "You have to call Josh and apologize. Maybe he'll put in a good word for you someplace if you show remorse."

Tinker, Samantha's two-year-old Chartreux cat, rubbed against Jenna's legs.

She reached down and picked him up, cuddling the sweet gray cat in her lap. She ran her fingers through his soft, warm fur. "I don't think so. Josh wouldn't lift a finger to help me. He didn't care a hoot that someone sent me a death threat. What kind of boss treats a person like that?"

"An angry one."

Jenna cringed. Josh's prediction that her days as an ad designer were over seemed to be coming true. She shook away the thought. "Something will turn up. I'm good at creating ads, and I don't need his endorsement.

My work speaks for itself." She had to stay positive. At least there hadn't been any more threats. Then again, how would she know? It wasn't like she could access her work e-mail.

"Did you try and find out if anyone at work had sent that e-mail as a joke?"

Samantha nodded. "No one claimed ownership."

"Figures. Why would they? If it was someone there, why cause more trouble when they already got away with it?" Jenna sincerely hoped it was someone from Ads by Design because the idea of a stranger sending her that creepy note had cost her a lot of sleep.

Maybe whoever had sent the scary message had cooled down. Never in her wildest imagination had she expected a person would turn on her like that. One thing was certain; she would not lose her cool in public again. What had she been thinking to spout off like that out in the open where the entire office could listen in? She couldn't have picked a more public place in their office to lose her temper.

Saying those things about Kratt Paper while at work had been a huge error in judgment, but that didn't mean they weren't true. Her former client's company was horrible on the environment and didn't care one bit about the public or the harm they were doing. Regardless, she should have kept her opinion to herself and not called them low-life money-grubbing shysters, even if it was true.

"Why won't you call, Josh? Tell him you were under

duress. He'll understand, considering how they trashed your pitch."

"No. I think banning me from the building was the final word in this situation."

Tinker purred as Jenna stroked his back. If only someone hadn't recorded that conversation and uploaded it to the Internet. She'd sure like to know who'd done it. One thing she did know was that someone at the ad agency had to have sent the threat. Jenna grabbed her phone again. She hadn't wanted to involve her parents, but it was time to swallow her pride and admit her failure. "Dad will help. He's the one who got me that job. Maybe he knows somebody looking for a person with my skills."

Samantha blew out her breath in a puff, causing her long bangs to fly up. "Right. I forgot the princess has a knight in shining armor for a dad."

Jenna crossed her arms and stared at her supposed friend. "Wow. That wasn't very nice. I thought you were on my side."

"I was. I am." She shook her head. "I'm sorry. I didn't mean to snap. Things at the office are tense, and I'm stressed. We've lost clients who don't want to be associated with our ad agency because of what you said."

Jenna bit her lip. "I'm really sorry. I don't know how to fix the damage. I'm sure it will blow over soon." She had to believe people would move their outrage to another situation. She ran her fingers through Tinker's coat, taking comfort in the feline's unconditional love.

What was she going to do about a job? She'd contacted everyone she knew in advertising, and no one would give her the time of day. She'd been at the top of her game until she'd opened her big mouth.

"Are you seriously going to call your dad? I know he has friends all over the area, but do you really want him pulling strings for you?"

Jenna hesitated. "You make it sound like a bad idea."

She shrugged. "I would think you'd want to find a job on your own. Personally, I wouldn't want my parents to know if I messed up like you did."

Ouch. Her former co-worker and friend was more than a little cranky today, but all things considered, Jenna could understand. Had she worn out her welcome? Probably. It had been an entire week, after all. It was definitely time to find a place to call home. "I'd rather they not know, but it's time to face reality. I need my parents."

She'd hoped to land another position right away, but now that her once exceptional reputation was in shreds that hadn't happened. She'd figured to rent an apartment near wherever she worked so she wouldn't need a car, but waiting to move might cause irreparable damage between her and Samantha.

"You're too quiet." Concern edged Samantha's voice. "What's going on in that head of yours?"

"I can't understand how my life could be destroyed

by a single moment captured on video by a vindictive colleague. The video was literally thirty seconds long. How can thirty seconds of stupidity destroy my life?"

Samantha's eyes widened. "Aren't you listening? It's not about just you. Ads by Design is having a public relations nightmare. SFW Software is threatening to pull their contract. You aren't the only one affected by your lapse in judgment. Words matter. You of all people should know that."

Jenna sighed. "Of course, I do. I'm sorry for the pity party. I didn't know things there were so bad."

"Polly was let go today."

Jenna gasped. "I thought Josh would assign her to the person who replaced me." Jenna swallowed the lump in her throat. "Poor Polly."

"He's letting people go, not hiring. We lost our biggest client, and things don't look good."

"I'm so sorry. If I could have a do-over I'd never have said those things." Regret and concern for Polly sickened her stomach. Jenna hadn't received so much as a text message from her former assistant. Polly had seemed indifferent to her departure, and that still hurt since her assistant had been the one person at Ads by Design who always had her back. Maybe she should reach out to the younger woman. "I should check on Polly."

She pressed her thumb to her smartphone then shot off a quick text. As the text whooshed away another came in, reminding her of her manicure scheduled for the following day. She'd cancel if she didn't need to have the next-to-impossible shellac polish taken off. She looked from her phone to Samantha who looked peeved.

"I wouldn't worry about Polly. She's smart and resourceful. Did you know she was my mentee when we were in college?"

"No. She never said a word."

"I guess she didn't want our relationship known." Samantha shrugged. "She was a freshman, and I was a fifth-year senior. To be honest, I didn't care much for Polly at first, but she grew on me. I actually encouraged her to go into advertising."

"I had no idea." She sucked in her bottom lip and stared at her phone, willing Polly to reply. "I hope she's okay. I feel really horrible that she got caught up in my mess."

Samantha waved a hand. "She'll bounce back. I imagine she'll have a new job by this time next week. I'm sorry for being so hard on you. Don't beat yourself up over her. And you know Josh. He built that business from nothing. Ads by Design will survive. We just might have a few rough months."

"Thanks. I hope you're right, but maybe I should try to fix the mess with Ads by Design anyway. I could call the local news stations and see if they'll interview me. I can give my side of the story and explain my frustration with a company that claims to be environmentally friendly and is the opposite."

"What good would that do except get you sued for libel?"

"It's not libelous if it's true."

"Doesn't matter. You must back pedal, or this will kill your career."

"It already has." Jenna gripped her phone tighter. "I'm taking a walk." She'd barely left the apartment in the week she'd been here, too afraid because of the threat, but she had to get out in the fresh air and think.

Jenna nudged Tinker. He hopped off her lap then leapt onto the windowsill.

"Don't forget your raincoat." Samantha motioned toward the hook on the wall beside the door.

"I won't." Jenna stood then grabbed it on her way out. She trotted down the stairs while slipping into her raincoat. She stepped outside, stopping under the awning, and then pushed air buds into her ears. She placed the call to her dad then slipped her phone into her pocket.

Steady light rain created puddles along the sidewalk. Would the rain ever give Seattle a break? The phone rang several times.

"How's my princess?"

She blew out the breath she'd been holding, "Hi, Dad." Her voice broke. She cleared her throat.

"Are you crying?" Concern filled Dad's voice.

She swiped at the dampness under her eyes. "Trying not to." Hearing his voice had been such a relief. She took a bracing breath. "I need to tell you something."

"Okay. I'm listening."

"I messed up, and now no one in the ad business will hire me—at least in Seattle." She stepped out from under the awning and walked with no destination in mind.

"I know. I saw you on the news."

"I made the news?" Horror shot through her. As if the viral video wasn't enough. "Wait. You knew, and you didn't call to check on me?" Her dad was her greatest champion. Sure, he had a big church to run, but he'd always been there for her.

"Your mom thought I should let you come to us on your own."

"Oh." That sounded like something Mom would say. She was more of a hands-off parent who let her learn by trial and error—not always the easiest or most pleasant way to grow.

"How are you doing, Princess? Have you found a job?"

"No. Which is why I'm calling. I need help. Being unemployed is the worst."

"I'm afraid you did that to yourself."

Her stomach lurched. "But what I said was true, even if it wasn't nice."

"True or not, you know better."

"You taught me to speak the truth." A car zipped through a puddle splashing water onto the sidewalk ahead of her.

"Speak truth in love. Not like what you did. Maybe

13

your mother's right, and I indulged you too much."

Speak truth in love? That sounded like the title of one of Dad's sermons. "No, you didn't. You've always made me feel special but not spoiled. How could that be wrong?"

"It's wrong because I forgot to mention that you are no more special than the homeless person on the street corner, except to your mother and me."

She pushed down her frustration. "Of course, I know that." Where was this coming from? Her dad had never been this harsh. He'd always been on her side. "For the record, that company everyone is so angry with me for bad-mouthing is polluting the Sound and who knows what else. All they care about is money. Isn't it okay to speak out when people are being hurt?"

"Of course it is, but we both know that wasn't the intent of your rant. It didn't help anyone."

She blew out her breath, feeling like an adolescent rather than a twenty-five-year-old woman. He was right, but what was she supposed to do now? The damage had been done. "You're right, and I'm sorry for what I said. If I could take it back, I would, but the damage is done, and now I need a job. Do you know anyone who might give me a chance?" Dad was her hero. He wouldn't let her down when it really mattered.

"I'm sorry, but I can't help you."

Jenna stopped. Someone bumped into her. She stepped out of the line of foot traffic. "I don't understand? You always help me. Don't you know of anyone looking for someone with my skills?"

"That's not the point. You need to find a job on your own this time. I have to go. There's a meeting in a minute. I'm afraid your video has upset some of the church board members as well. I'll be praying for you."

"Okay. Bye." She pocketed her phone. Would her dad lose his job, too? She sank onto a bench. What had she done?

2

Rain pelted Carissa Jones' jacket as she walked beside her latest client, Jason Wood, the owner of SFW Software. Though a powerful man, he didn't have an imposing presence at five foot ten with a medium build and dark, clean-cut hair. He was all business right down to his wingtip shoes.

She'd give about anything for sunshine, but all things considered, the gloom was fitting. "Pick up the pace, Jason. I don't like you being out in the open like this. You're an easy target." His SUV sat parked about one hundred feet away, thanks to the ridiculously long path into the building from the parking lot.

"Anyone ever tell you your bedside manner needs some work?" Jason increased his stride.

"Sorry. Next time I'll watch from the rooftop and let Marc walk you to your car." She was in no mood for attitude. The threat on her client was serious. She wished her entire team was here right now, but Jason had insisted on only one bodyguard at his side.

He chuckled. "It's fine. I'm just on edge."

She caught movement in the bushes to their right and put her hand out to stop her client. A cat darted from the bush. She blew out a breath. "Hustle." She picked up her pace. Her hair stood on the back of her neck—something wasn't right, but she couldn't see anything.

A shot rang out. She tackled her client to the ground smacking the hard cement with her forearm. A bullet whizzed past her ear. She sucked in a breath as she tapped the button on her wrist and spoke into the mic. "Marc, shot came from the east side. Parking garage roof."

Jason groaned from beneath her and fought to move.

"Stay put if you want to live."

"I see him," Marc Olsen said, his voice coming through her earpiece.

A single shot fired in the distance. Sirens screamed. Praise God someone had called 9-1-1. She'd been too busy to do so herself.

"Got him," Marc said. "Stand by. Moving closer to confirm."

Carissa had no doubt Marc hit his target. He was a crack shot and never missed. She rolled off Jason.

Footsteps raced toward them. Carissa's pulse thrummed in her ears. She reached for her Glock as she turned. She blew out a breath. "It's only one of your security guards. You okay?"

The thirty-year-old tech giant pushed to his hands and knees. "I think so. Am I safe now?"

"We can hope. The police will be here any minute to take your statement." She studied Jason's pallor. "Take it easy getting up. I don't want you to pass out."

The security guard reached out a hand to help his boss stand. "Are you okay, Mr. Wood?"

"The bullet missed me."

"That's great news. When I saw what happened, I called the police and rushed out here."

"Thank you, George."

Jason looked at Carissa. "What if there's another shooter? He might not miss this time."

"You'd already be dead if there was."

He leaned to one side.

Carissa reached out to steady him. "Easy now." An ambulance pulled to a stop nearby with a police cruiser right behind it. "Why don't you sit here for a few minutes while I talk with the authorities? George, will you help him?"

"Of course. Come on, Mr. Wood."

Carissa approached Officer Dillon Brady—a good man and an excellent cop. They'd run across one another more than once since they started Protection Inc. in Seattle.

"What's going on, Carissa? We had a report of shots fired. Happened to be a block over when the call came in."

"Someone shot at my client."

Officer Brady looked beyond Carissa. "Jason Wood is your client?" He whistled long and low. "He okay?"

"Other than being shaken up, he's fine. He had a credible threat made against him last week. My company was hired to protect him."

"Looks like you did your job. What about the shooter?"

"Marc shot him. His condition is still unknown. Everything happened fast."

"It usually does." He wrote something on his notepad.

She tapped her earpiece. "Status report, Marc?"

"Almost to the roof now. Stand by."

Carissa closed her eyes. *Lord, please let this be over.* As much as she liked her job, it came with a fair amount of stress, and people shooting at clients ranked at the top of her stress level. Marc had been positioned on the rooftop of SFW Software, watching for trouble. Thank goodness, he was able to spot the shooter on the parking garage roof across the street from them.

She pointed to the garage to their east. "The shooter was up there. My associate is on his way to check on him."

Marc's voice sounded in her ear. "We have a problem."

"What?"

"He's gone, and there's a trail of blood."

Her gut clenched. This wasn't over. Carissa relayed the news to Officer Brady.

19

He spoke into the radio on his shoulder. A moment later, he returned his attention to Carissa. "You better get your client out of here. I'll be in touch with Marc for his statement. In the meantime, the area hospitals are being alerted to be on the lookout for a gunshot victim."

Carissa nodded. She strode to Jason, who now sat on the edge of the ambulance, between the open doors. "We need to move."

"Okay." He turned to the medics. "Thanks for your help." He held an ice pack to his chin that must have made contact with the concrete when she'd tackled him.

Carissa tapped her earpiece. "I'm taking Jason to Protection Inc.'s office until the shooter's found."

"When I'm done talking with the police, I'll join you."

She saw her client safely to her car and pulled away from the tech giant's building.

Jason gripped the door. "Why can't we go to *my* office? It's closer."

"We don't know where the threat is coming from. Your place is too big to secure properly."

"Are you suggesting one of my own people wants me dead?"

"It's possible."

He crossed his arms. "I don't think it's related to SFW Software."

"Why not?"

"It's a little known fact that I'm chairman of the

board at Kratt Paper."

"The company that made the news?"

"One and the same." He frowned. "I ought to sue that ad woman we hired for defamation, but from what I've heard, she's been blackballed from every ad agency within a hundred-mile radius of Seattle. We'll recover."

"How is it you run and operate SFW Software and chair the board at a paper company?"

"Long story short, my wife's family owns Kratt Paper. They wanted a known figurehead at the helm. I agreed."

"How do you have the time?"

"I delegate well, and the board only meets once a month."

"So you don't own Kratt Paper?"

"Correct. But I'm the face of the company as far as anyone's concerned."

"Why didn't you disclose this when you hired us?" She shot him a frustrated look. It would have been helpful to know that sooner. They'd assumed the threat was related to the software company and had spent time and resources based on that assumption. "You could have died today. If you'd been upfront from the beginning, we might have been able to avoid what happened."

"I don't see how. What would have changed?"

"The focus of our investigation. You knew our team was working behind the scenes to find who had threatened you." Anger coursed through her. Some people were their own worst enemies. She glanced in her rearview mirror. No one appeared to follow them. At least there was one thing to be thankful for.

Carissa stood in Frank Davis's office beside Marc, her business partner and boyfriend. Even after a couple months of being a couple, it still felt odd referring to him as her boyfriend. Jason sat in the bullpen with Sally Wilson, currently their only other bodyguard.

Marc nudged her shoulder. "Stop daydreaming."

Carissa shook her head. "I'm not."

Frank scowled. "It's time to hire another person. We have our hands full with the Wood case, and we have other jobs we're committed to."

Carissa blew out a breath. Their services were in high demand. They protected anyone from stalking victims to celebrities and even hired out as event security. There was a surprisingly large need for bodyguards and security details. "I thought after we brought on Sally that would be it for a while."

Marc chuckled. "What do you have against hiring someone new?"

She frowned. "I don't like to shake up things. We work well together. A new person might mess that up, but I agree we need someone else."

Frank's eyes narrowed. "You agree? What's up with that?"

"Come on, guys. Give me a break. I'm not blind. We need more help. There I said it. Move on."

Marc and Frank both chuckled.

"Don't gloat." A smile escaped, and she ducked her chin.

Marc reached out and gently tipped up her chin. "We wouldn't dream of it." He winked.

Her heart melted at the love that shone in his eyes. "So tell me about this candidate, Frank."

"Cop from Portland, Oregon. Name's Peter King."

"Send me his resumé." She planted a peck on Marc's cheek. "I'm meeting a potential client at Gently Brewed, a coffee shop."

"Seriously? Aren't you forgetting about someone? We already have a client." Frank motioned toward Jason who sat at Sally's desk talking on his phone.

"I realize that, but I made a promise. Jason can wait here for us to return. He's content using our office to handle his work. I try to keep my promises. It won't take long. Besides, I don't have to accept the case."

Marc glanced at Frank then Carissa. "Who are you meeting?"

"One of the baristas. She thinks a customer might be stalking her."

"Why?" he badgered.

"That's what I'm going to find out. She says he's there all the time, so I want to see him for myself."

Marc rubbed the back of his neck. "I'll join you. You never know when something could go south.

Frank and Sally can handle things here for a bit."

Carissa gave his hand a squeeze. "Not necessary. I don't think I'll have a problem. Besides, it's a coffee shop. You hate coffee. I can handle this."

"No doubt, but while the two of you are talking, I'll keep an eye on this person, assuming he's there."

She sighed. "Fine. You'd better leave now then, because she's expecting me in five minutes. I'd rather not walk in together."

He saluted her and marched out.

She chuckled and glanced at Frank. "What?"

Frank raised his hands palms out. "Nothing. Just enjoying the scene. I feel like a proud father."

Carissa rolled her eyes. "See you later, *Dad*." Frank was like a father at times, but in reality, they were former partners from their days as cops. They'd meshed well and decided to go into business together.

She strolled out and nodded to Sally. The thirty-something, medium-build brunette had been a smart hire. They had a lot in common too, including their mutual love for exceptional coffee and former careers as police officers. "Everything okay?"

"Yep. When you have a few minutes, I'd like to run something by you."

"You got it. Give me an hour." Maybe by then the police would locate the man Marc wounded, and they could wrap up the Wood case.

Marc sat in a corner booth at Gently Brewed. The orange wall color gave it a warm and homey feel. He held a cup of something the barista had recommended for people who weren't coffee drinkers. It was a far cry from the soda he usually drank, but it served its purpose as a prop.

The door to the shop opened, and Carissa walked in. She smiled at a college-age woman with bright red hair that hung to her chin. The young woman motioned to a table on the opposite side of the room from him then grabbed two cups from the counter and joined her.

He studied the people in the room. Two businessmen sat at a small table near the door. A harried mother and her toddler were seated at a table along the wall near Carissa and her potential client. A twenty-something guy sat with his back to the window and a laptop open in front of him, but he wasn't typing. Instead his attention was on the baristas working behind the counter. Why sit by the window if he didn't want to look outside, especially when the light from the window would cause a glare on the computer screen?

He glanced toward Carissa and her client who kept looking over at the computer guy. Could Computer Guy be the problem? It wouldn't surprise him. He probably had a crush on one of the baristas. Maybe a word with him would make this problem go away. He started to rise then thought better of it. Carissa would not appreciate him butting in.

Carissa stood, carrying her cup, and approached the guy.

Marc stood and moved to a closer table. He couldn't miss whatever it was she would say.

"Excuse me." Carissa stood blocking the guy's view of the baristas.

The man grinned as his eyes roamed her body.

Marc clenched and unclenched his fingers. "Keep your eyes to yourself, buddy," he muttered under his breath. He took a sip from the cup, never taking his gaze off Carissa and Computer Guy. He choked on the chocolate and coffee tasting brew, forgetting it wasn't his usual soda and spewed the coffee all over the table.

Carissa looked in his direction.

"Sorry. Too hot." Not true. The barista was sorely mistaken about that drink. How did people drink that stuff? He grabbed a napkin and wiped up the mess then refocused his attention on Carissa.

"May I join you?" Carissa asked Computer Guy.

"Uh. Sure." He closed his laptop and moved it to a messenger-style bag.

"This is my hangout, so when my friends," she motioned toward the counter where a couple of young women served customers, "told me about you, I decided to make it official."

He sipped from his large drink. "Make what official?"

"I want to make you aware of how sitting here every day for hours, facing the baristas and watching them work makes them feel."

"Huh?" His brow scrunched.

"They feel stalked."

His face turned red. "Oh. No. That's not…" He shook his head and glanced nervously toward the counter. "I'm not a stalker. I'm working on a movie. My heroine is a barista."

"I see. I enjoy movies. May I see your script?"

He laughed.

She didn't.

He sobered. "Oh. You're serious. You really want to see it." He bent over and pulled out his laptop again. "I can't believe this is happening. I need to write this into the movie." His fingers flew across the keys then he turned the screen to face Carissa.

A moment later, Carissa stood. "Thanks for sharing that with me, but you should probably find a different coffee shop every day. That way no one will feel threatened by your research."

He stood. "Message received. I'll leave now. Please tell the baristas I'm sorry and no harm meant." He rushed from Gently Brewed.

Carissa turned and headed back to the woman she'd been speaking with moments ago. She spoke softly to the woman then quickly joined him. "I assume you heard my conversation with the screenwriter."

"Yep. So you believed him?"

"Yes. Hannah said his name is Willy, and she confirmed he is a screenplay writer. Apparently, she's spoken with him about it. Anyway, the screenplay I saw looked legit. The quick glance I took showed a scene in a coffee shop. I think he legitimately was here observing how things are done. His downfall was coming back to the same place every day."

"Maybe they're his muses. What if he comes back again?"

She shrugged. "If he does, I told Hannah to call me." She stood. "You ready to head to the office?"

"In a minute." He motioned for her to sit.

She sunk back onto the chair. "What's up? We really should get back. Jason can be a pain, and I don't want to give Sally any reason to quit."

"She'll survive five extra minutes. I miss you. We've been working so much lately we haven't had any time to ourselves."

"We see each other every day."

"It's not the same. Once we get the new guy settled, we should take some time off and hang out—just you and me—like we did after we finished that job in Oregon a couple of months ago."

A soft smile raised her lips. "I'd like that. Let's put it on the calendar for…June."

"June? That's months and months away."

She chuckled. "We have several events we're doing security for between now and then, and you know how Frank takes on emergency cases. We'd be lucky to get time off that coincides."

He nodded. "We should close for two weeks at Christmas. That's only a couple of months away." He should have thought of that sooner.

"Maybe. We could float the idea by Frank."

"If we take a vote it'd be two to one." He liked those odds, assuming Carissa voted to take time off. Since he'd been a part of Protection Inc. they'd handled too many jobs to count, including a couple stalking cases. It appeared they were all married to their jobs and seemed to be constantly working. Were it not for their partnership, he'd never get to see Carissa—another reason they needed to bring in an additional bodyguard or two.

Carissa stood. "Come on. I don't want Frank to hire anyone without our having a say in the decision."

Carissa pulled up a chair to Sally's desk. Marc had taken their client home and would be on guard duty tonight. "Sorry it took me half the day to get back to you. What's going on?"

Sally glanced toward the new guy they'd hired moments ago and raised her brows.

"Peter King is the latest addition to Protection Inc. He's a former cop. I think you'll like him. I was impressed."

Sally's eyes widened. "That's saying a lot coming from you."

Carissa chuckled. "I'm sorry if I've been a little hard on you."

"It's fine. I always know where I stand. I respect that."

Carissa had liked Sally from day one. The woman was exceptional at her job. "What do you want to run by me?"

"I've been thinking about Protection Inc. and how we need to have a little fun once in a while."

"Fun? At work? I don't understand."

Sally chuckled. "That's because you eat, sleep, and breathe this job. But a little fun now and then builds camaraderie. Plus, we've all been working so hard that I'm afraid if we don't take a timeout for some fun we'll burn out."

Marc had said something similar earlier today, though it had been geared to alone time with him. Maybe a little entertainment was what they all needed. She certainly didn't want Frank, Marc, or Sally to walk away from the company. "What'd you have in mind?"

"An escape room." Her face lit. "There's one not far from here. We could do it on our lunch break or after work one day."

Carissa coughed, holding back a laugh when she realized Sally was totally serious. "Sorry. Umm…you don't think that will feel like work?" Following clues to get out of a locked room in under a certain amount of time did not sound like fun.

"How do you figure that as work? We protect people. We don't solve riddles and follow clues." She crossed her arms. "Well, at least not for the joy of it."

"I'll run it by the men and see what they say. If they're up for it, we'll put it on the calendar. Maybe we could do it for our Christmas party in December."

"That's a couple of months away."

"We'll have something to look forward to." Carissa held her breath, hoping this would appease Sally.

Sally grinned. "Sounds like a plan then. How'd it go at Gently Brewed earlier?"

"Better than expected. I think I nipped that situation in the bud."

"Good for you." Sally turned back to her computer. "I need to finish this report for Frank then head home and get prepared for tomorrow."

Carissa stood. She'd better get that escape room on the calendar and talk with Frank about a break at Christmas. She realized the bad guys didn't take a holiday, but Protection Inc. had been working non-stop for two solid months.

She passed Marc who raised a brow. "Going to talk with Frank about what we discussed. Want to join?"

"I wish." He lowered his voice. "I need to take Jason back to his office. He has a meeting he's throwing a fit about."

"The police didn't find the man you wounded?"

"Not yet. He's bound to turn up. Based on the blood trail, he needed stitches at the very least."

She nodded. "Wish me luck." Frank had given them a couple of weeks off in August. He might balk at the idea of two more only four months later. She squared her shoulders and marched into her business partner's office. "You have a minute?"

Frank motioned to an empty chair.

She spelled out her plan.

"I like it." He sat back and laced his fingers behind his head.

"You do?" She narrowed her eyes. "Why?"

He laughed. "I realize we had a break not long ago, but we work crazy hours with infrequent days off. I'm not an ogre. I realize we all need time to decompress from our heavy workload, and the week before and after Christmas is perfect. I'll clear the calendar."

"What about the escape room?"

"Negative. You and Sally could go to it, but count me out."

Carissa stood. She wouldn't push. At least not right now. Marc would be thrilled with Frank's concession.

3

Peter King hoisted a box from the rental truck and headed inside to his storage unit. Good thing this was the last box. His back had suffered enough. Normally, only inactivity set off his nagging injury, but apparently, moving boxes did too. Oh well, there was nothing he could do about it. He'd probably be making several trips to this place until he found a permanent home. Living out of a suitcase at a hotel wasn't his idea of a good time—at least he had a job. Now he needed to find a place to live.

He turned and bumped into someone.

"Ooph," a woman exhaled.

He lowered the box. "I'm sorry. Are you okay?" His eyes widened. A woman who looked to be in her middle-twenties with long, silky hair the color of his favorite dark espresso stared back at him with big brown, sad-looking eyes.

She blinked rapidly. "I'm fine." She held open the door. "After you."

His phone vibrated in his pocket. He lowered the box. "Thanks, but I should take this call."

She nodded and disappeared inside.

"Peter here."

"It's Frank. Check your e-mail. I sent you the file. It lays out your job duties for a gig on Friday night."

Peter grinned. "Thanks. I'll be sure to study it." Good thing his new boss had called with a heads-up. He rarely checked e-mail.

"You getting settled?"

"Working on it."

"Good. Catch you later."

Peter pocketed his phone, hoisted the box into his arms, then went inside. This place was a maze, but thankfully, he'd figured out the route to his unit. He passed by an open door that had been closed on his previous trips inside. The woman from earlier sat in a storage unit a quarter the size of his on a folding chair, staring at the delicate-looking tiara in her hand. Behind her was a tower of precariously stacked boxes. Clearly, she didn't have a clue about physics.

She looked up and quickly swiped at her eyes.

Had she been crying? "It's a little early to be digging out your Halloween costume." He grinned, hoping to lighten the moment.

She tossed the tiara aside. "Just chasing memories."

Why would a tiara make her cry? "Not good ones by the look of it."

"Mixed is more like it." She swiped at a fresh tear.

Maybe he should keep his observations to himself. "I don't want to interrupt. I'll leave you to your memories." He walked away. That woman was clearly troubled. He couldn't help wondering why. She was beautiful, and if he hadn't seen how sad she was, he'd have believed her life was perfect. He opened the door to his unit and slid the final box onto the stack that reached the top of his shoulders.

A yelp pierced the air. He turned and ran toward the sound, ignoring the pain in his back.

The woman from earlier lay buried under what had once been stacked boxes.

She moaned.

"Are you okay?" He stepped into the small unit.

"I think so." She slid her arm out from a box that had 'throw pillows' printed in black ink across it. "I was in such a rush when I brought my stuff here. I think I misjudged the placement of some boxes."

He almost laughed. However this wasn't a laughing matter. "Do you need help?"

She sat up. "More than you can possibly imagine, but I guess you meant the boxes." She yanked her legs free then rolled over to her hands and knees and stood.

"You're bleeding." He motioned to her arm. "There's a first aid kit in the glove box of my rental truck."

She looked down and frowned. "Thanks. That's really nice of you. It seems I can't catch a break."

"Come again?" He walked beside her toward the main doors.

"I've had a really bad past week or so." She shook her head. "I'm losing track of time."

"It can't be that bad. I'm sure there's an upside." When had he become Pollyanna? That role had generally been reserved for his late Aunt Charlotte.

"I assure you it is. I ruined my life and the lives of people I care about."

"That sounds serious. Why not tell me about it while we get you patched up?"

"You don't want to hear my problems."

"Talking often helps. You have an impartial listener." He waited for her to start toward him before turning and heading to the exit. It'd been his experience that women liked to vent, and all he had to do was listen.

They stepped out into the hazy sunshine. He went to the cab of the truck, reached into the glove box for the first aid kit, and pulled it out. "I'm sure there's an alcohol swab and a bandage in here somewhere."

"I lost my job, my home, and my car," she blurted. "Then I found out I might have cost my dad his job—oh, and my assistant was let go. Not to mention someone might want me dead. I'm a walking disaster. Better not get too close, or who knows what will happen to you."

He sure hadn't expected to hear any of that. "Whoa. I'm sorry you're dealing with so much, but don't you think you might be exaggerating a bit?" He pulled out the alcohol swab and handed it to her. "What makes you think someone wants you dead?"

36

"Thanks." She wiped the cut, cleaning away the blood, and then stuffed the used wipe into the pouch it'd come from. "An e-mail."

He handed her a bandage. "It doesn't look too bad."

"It's only a scratch."

It was more than that, but didn't appear to need stitches. Not that he was a trained medical professional, but it really wasn't bad. "So what are you going to do about the e-mail?"

"Nothing. I can't get it out of my head, but since nothing more has happened, I want to believe it was a sick joke."

"Why would someone do that?"

She shrugged. "To scare me I suppose. It worked too."

"What did the e-mail say?"

"It was a picture of a woman floating face down in a body of water with a message in red that, said 'this could be you.'" She shrugged. "A few minutes after receiving the e-mail, I was fired because of something I said about a company that's polluting the Sound. Symbolism at its best, yet I still can't shake the feeling I could be in danger."

She wasn't exaggerating. "Did you notify the police?"

"No. I'm sure they have much more important things to deal with. Like I said, it was probably a bad joke."

Didn't she realize she could be in serious danger? "I hope you're right. But you might want to consider that the threat could be legit. I'd hate for anything to happen to you."

"I'll take that under advisement. I guess I should clean up the mess. Thanks for your help." She smiled sweetly at him.

Her trusting brown eyes endeared her to him, reminding him of his Aunt Charlotte. He hesitated. "I'd be happy to help with the boxes." What was he doing? The last thing he needed was to get involved with her problems. He left trouble behind when he moved to Seattle and had no intention of finding more here, but his need to protect and serve had him wanting to get involved. "I have to go inside anyway. When I heard you yelp, I left my unit open."

She gave a wobbly smile. "Thanks for coming to my rescue."

He opened the door to the storage facility. "Anyone would have." His aunt had instilled in him the importance of helping those in need.

"Nonetheless, thank you. By the way, I'm Jenna."

"Peter." He retraced his steps. It would only take a few minutes to stack her boxes since there hadn't been many. He put the heaviest boxes on the bottom.

She stood in the doorway and watched. "What do you do?"

"Retired cop." The words popped out before he could say bodyguard.

"Retired? But you can't be more than thirty."

"We all have our baggage." He nodded toward her boxes. "Some more obvious than others."

A hint of a smile touched her lips. "So, you don't work?"

He stacked the last box, making sure it wouldn't topple. "I start my new career tomorrow." He nodded and brushed past her. "You really should file a police report about that e-mail."

"It had to be a joke."

"I'm not laughing. In my experience, this person could be dangerous. I know someone who could look into it for you."

She tilted her head to the side as if thinking over his offer. "I appreciate your concern, but I'm going to pass. Thanks, though."

"Sure thing. I hope your day improves."

"I hope my life improves," she muttered.

He hesitated. No. She'd turned down his offer for help with the threatening e-mail. He would not get involved. Trying to help a woman in need was what got him into trouble before and what ultimately caused his injury, forcing him into an early retirement from the police force. Seattle was his second chance—a new beginning. He would not mess it up.

4

Marc eased into a seat in the corner of Jason Wood's office. The man he'd wounded had yet to be found, so they were still on protection detail. This job had grown old fast. He much preferred outdoor gigs. Sitting in a stuffy office about put him to sleep.

Carissa would be nearby except she was on some kind of bonding outing with Sally. Apparently, Sally wanted to do an escape room—not his thing, but if it raised employee morale, he was all for it—even if it meant working alone for a few hours.

A commotion in the reception area grabbed his attention. Would anyone be foolish enough to try something during business hours? Marc drew his Glock and stood. "Get down behind your desk and stay quiet," he whispered.

Jason did as Marc ordered without hesitation.

Marc stole over to the door and opened it a crack. A man stood in front of the receptionist, a gun in his hand. The receptionist stood firmly in place to the side of her desk.

Marc weighed his options. If he stepped out of the room, it might escalate the danger to Jason's staff, mostly the brave woman.

Marc closed the office door and called 9-1-1 to relay the situation then cracked the door again. Should he engage or stay with his client? If Carissa were here, she would say stay with the client—only engage when necessary.

It appeared the man he'd shot had a contact in the medical field since he'd not been reported by any hospitals, and he didn't look too worse for wear. He must have had his wound cleaned, stitched, and dressed.

"I demand you let me see him! He's responsible for polluting the Sound. He needs to pay for what he's done." The man shouted and waved the gun at Jason's receptionist, who had not moved and continued blocking the access to Jason's office. She was a larger woman, but he doubted she could stop the man if he got physical The woman wasn't backing down despite the weapon in the man's hand.

"Sir, Mr. Wood has nothing to do with that. You have the wrong person."

The man slowed his motions and lowered his arm. "He's named as the head of their board."

"I've heard that too, but I can assure you, my boss would never do what you're accusing him of."

Marc eased the door closed. If he stepped out of the room, he'd agitate the man more and most likely get the receptionist and himself shot and leave Jason unguarded. He needed to allow law enforcement to diffuse the situation. "Is there another way out of here?"

"No," Jason said. "Is it the same person who shot at me?"

"I believe so." He'd seen him though a scope but not up close and personal like this. "How'd he get past security?"

"Beats me, but assuming you get me out of this alive, they're all fired."

Marc frowned. Assuming they were still alive, they deserved to be let go. "Your safety is my top priority. He's not getting through those doors without bodily harm."

More shouting sounded from the reception area. He pulled the door a crack and breathed easier. Two security officers stood with pistols aimed at the threat who was on his knees with his fingers laced behind his head. "They got him, Jason." He took a calming breath. That had been too close for comfort. Satisfied the danger had passed, he turned to face his client.

Jason stood, ashen-faced, resting his palms on his desk. "I'm so glad this is finally over."

"You okay?"

"Just collecting myself before going out there."

"You're staying right here until the police arrive."

Confusion filled Jason's face. "If the police didn't stop him, who did?"

"Your security. Not sure how he got past them, but they're here now and took care of him."

His client ran a shaky hand through his hair and sank onto his desk chair. "Good. Maybe I won't fire them after all." He tilted his head. "Now what?"

Marc glanced out the door again. Officer Brady, along with three other police officers, were in the reception area. "Guess, we'll find out soon. Stay put. I'll be right back."

He opened the door far enough to slide through the opening. "Officer Brady, we meet again."

"Wish it was under better circumstances. I heard the call and decided to assist, considering what happened the last time a call came from this address. Your client okay?"

"Yes." *Thank the Lord.* He could have handled the situation if needed, but he was glad he didn't have to.

Officer Brady walked over to the doorway of Jason's office and lowered his voice. "Is that the man who shot at your client?"

He nodded. "I believe so. If he is, he should have a gunshot wound."

"He looks to be in good shape for having been shot recently." He turned back to the other officer who had accompanied him. "Does he have a gunshot wound?" He turned to Marc. "Where would it be?"

"Left shoulder area."

The guy sucked in a sharp breath when the other officer touched his shoulder. "Watch it. I admit it. I shot at him. He deserves to die for his crimes against the Sound."

Officer Brady furrowed his brows. "I'd like to speak with your client."

Marc led the way into the office. "Jason, you remember Officer Brady."

"Of course. Thanks for coming."

"I have some questions."

"I'm sure you do. Give me one sec." Jason's gaze moved to Marc. "Thank you for everything you've done." He seemed to stand taller. "I'm glad this is over. You and your team were fantastic. Send me a bill. You were worth every penny. That's one bill I won't mind paying. Since my life is no longer in danger, I'll no longer need your services. As of now, consider yourself relieved of duty."

Marc nodded then spoke softly to Officer Brady. "Was he working alone?"

"Unknown at this time. I'll keep you apprised."

"Appreciate it." He left without a backward glance. Jason knew how to reach the team if he had a problem.

Jenna gazed at her hand as Suzie, her long-time manicurist, filed her nails. The upscale spa was as busy as usual with every nail tech working on a client. She would go without polish for a change. She certainly couldn't afford to waste money on a shellac manicure without a job and no prospects. Sure, she had some savings, but this was a frivolity now. When she'd made the appointment, she'd been gainfully employed and considered it a professional necessity.

"You're quiet today. Is everything okay?" Suzie moved on to her other hand.

"Not really," she kept her voice low. "Things have been rough lately." Suzie's kind demeanor and excellent manicures were the reason she'd been coming to her since she had started her job at Ads by Design. The woman didn't seem to have a mean bone in her body, which was refreshing, considering how everyone trampled all over each other to get ahead where she'd worked.

"Ah, sweetie. I'm really sorry to hear that. Is that why you're foregoing the shellac?"

"Yes. The upkeep is too much for me since I lost my job." It was painful to admit, but Suzie would never make her feel bad about it, nor was she a gossip. Not once had she heard the thirty-something woman talking about another person when she was in the salon.

"I understand. I hope things look up soon."

"Thanks. You really don't know about what's been going on with me?"

Suzie shook her head. "How would I?"

"It made the news."

Suzie's eyes widened, and she stopped working for a second before regaining her composure. "I don't watch much television, and I definitely don't watch the news—too much negativity. Besides, I spend my evenings chauffeuring my son and daughter. Between

45

piano lessons, swim lessons, and church activities, I feel like all I do is work and run kids around. At least waiting on them gives me time to read."

How had she not known Suzie was a mom?

"Excuse me." The woman getting a manicure to her right smiled. Her strawberry blonde hair hung in perfect waves, framing her face. "I couldn't help overhearing your situation. As it happens, I might be able to help."

Jenna's insides leapt. "Seriously? How?"

"I'm Brandi Parker." She slipped an unpolished hand into her purse and pulled out a business card. "I started my own ad agency a few months ago. My client list is growing steadily, and I could use someone part time. I'd be happy to look at your resumé."

"Oh. That's really nice, but I need a fulltime position with benefits."

Brandi raised a perfectly manicured brow. "As it happens, I'm familiar with your situation. I don't think you'll get a better offer. Keep my card. If you change your mind, give me a call. I'm not posting the position for another couple of weeks, so there's time."

Jenna's face heated. "Sure. Thanks." Jenna dropped the card into her Coach purse. She turned back to Brandi. "Why are you willing to consider me when no one else will even take my calls?"

"I believe in second chances. Plus, I've built my business on my solid reputation. My clients trust me, but you…" she dragged out the word. "Let's just say, I believe I can help."

"They wouldn't trust me without you backing me is what you're insinuating." The truth struck deep. Had she really fallen so low that the average advertiser wouldn't want to work with her?

"It's possible they wouldn't, but if we work together, I think they might. That being said, for this to work, you'd have to sign a contract with the conditions of your employment. If you've reconsidered my offer, we could give it a test-run. See how we work together."

"What kind of contract?" Would other firms want the same thing from her?

"Nothing major. But I'd need it in writing that you wouldn't bad mouth any of our clients, and if caught doing so, it would be grounds for immediate termination. You would also need to stay off social media."

"No social media?" Was that even legal?

"Once trust is built between us, we could re-visit the social media clause."

Suzie cleared her throat. "All done."

Jenna looked down at her bare nails and swallowed the lump in her throat. Her life had been reduced to naked nails and ridiculous contracts. Well, she could at least control one thing. She paid Suzie then stood. "It was nice meeting you, Brandi. I appreciate the job offer, but I really need full-time work. Best of luck with your business."

If Brandi was surprised by the rejection, she didn't show it. In fact, it almost looked like the woman pitied her. She didn't need or want anyone's pity. Something would turn up. She walked out of the shop and headed for the bus—her new mode of transportation. Footsteps behind her caused her to look over her shoulder—no one. A chill rushed through her, and she quickened her steps.

Friday evening, Peter stood atop a building on the south side of Seattle, holding binoculars to his eyes. Protection Inc. was covering an outdoor concert this evening. His job was to watch for trouble while the rest of the team guarded the band near the stage. Their lead singer and front man had a credible threat made against him, specifically for this concert. It wasn't police work, but he'd moonlighted as a bodyguard many times, as well as served as extra security at events. This wasn't all that different.

He hadn't been able to shake thoughts of the woman he'd met at the storage unit. He regretted not asking for her number after telling Frank about her. He was very concerned for her and suggested there was room for anyone in need of their services. No wonder they were so busy at Protection Inc. At least now he had a supply of business cards to hand out to people in need of their services.

The roar from the crowd increased in volume until he wished for earplugs even atop the building. He focused his gaze on the stage. The band struck their first chord. A man wearing all black pushed through the crowd. Normally, they'd be wired to speak to one another, but with this being a loud concert, they were depending on text messages—not the most reliable. He sent a warning about the man to the ground team.

Frank, the boss who always seemed in charge, sent the signal that the message was received. A minute later, he diverted the man away from the stage.

A text lit his phone screen. *We got him. Keep your eyes open. Might not be working alone.*

Peter held the binoculars to his eyes and scanned the crowd once again. Everyone appeared to be enjoying the music, and no one in particular stood out. He checked his watch. It would be a long night.

He needed to prove himself to his bosses with this first assignment, especially since Frank and Carissa were former cops too. He didn't want to let them down. From his best guess, Frank had served ten to fifteen years more than Peter had.

He hadn't planned to retire early, but a push out of a second story window had done a number on his back, making it impossible for him to perform the duties of his job as a beat cop. He shook away the disturbing memory.

A commotion stage right drew his attention. Sally had a guy on the ground with her knee in his back. What had he missed? He was sure to hear about it, whatever it was.

He walked to the opposite edge of the building for a different view and to loosen his back muscles. The outskirts of the concert crowd were relatively quiet. A lone woman walked along the sidewalk. Wait a minute—he held the binoculars to his eyes. The woman from the storage unit walked with hunched shoulders. She must live in the area. Several apartment and condo complexes were nearby. He stood on the roof of one.

A twinge of guilt pricked at him. He should have pushed her harder to find out her story—forget that he didn't need or want to get involved. He was driven by the need to protect others. He tore his gaze away as she entered a building, and he got back to work.

Two hours later, the concertgoers had vacated the park, the stage was nearly cleared, and the band had loaded onto their bus. Their job would be done once the bus drove away. The diesel engine roared to life.

Marc walked over to him, his long legs covering the space quickly. "Good job tonight. The local police took the man you spotted into custody. Frank said that he was the one who'd made the threat."

Peter nodded. "What about the person Sally had pinned to the ground?"

"An over-exuberant fan who tried to get onto the stage."

"It takes all kinds I guess."

Marc chuckled. "You're going to fit in well."

"Thanks." At six foot and clearly quite familiar with the weight room, his boss could be intimidating, but he didn't intimidate Peter. They had hit it off immediately. Frank and Carissa were a different story. Frank was more reserved in his praise and Carissa…? He wasn't sure about her yet.

Frank strode over to them. "How's the back?"

"Fine." It hurt, but so long as it wasn't spasming, he could manage.

"Don't lie to me." Frank scowled.

"Wouldn't dream of it. I'm still moving. It's fine."

Frank's face relaxed. "Good. Go home. We have the weekend off. Our weekend job cancelled. Be at the office at nine Monday morning."

"Yes, sir." He waved to Sally and Carissa then walked the block and a half to where he'd parked his Ford Escape.

He'd located an apartment earlier today. Thankfully, it wasn't near this park. He'd hate having to listen to a concert every Friday night during the summer and early fall months. Not that he had anything against music. He simply appreciated quiet when he wasn't working.

A commotion coming from inside the building snagged his attention. He looked to his right into the lit lobby, the same one the woman from the storage unit had entered. His eyes widened—Jenna. He pulled open the glass door and entered the lobby. "Everything okay?"

The man who'd been shouting at her stopped and glared at him. "Who are you?"

"A friend of Jenna's. What's going on?"

"It's between us."

Jenna's pale face had him moving toward her. He put himself between Jenna and the man. "It's late."

The man's lip curled. "Mind your own business."

Peter pulled his shoulders back and straightened to his full five-foot-eleven height. He'd spent many hours in the weight room rehabilitating his back and had the biceps to prove it. Maybe that's why he and Marc had hit it off so easily.

The man backed away. "Whatever. Next time pay attention to where you're going." He pointed at Jenna then turned and strode from the building.

Peter watched the man leave then turned to face her. "What was that all about?"

"I walked out in front of his car at an intersection, and he followed me here. I had gone up to my friend's apartment then remembered I'd forgotten she asked me to collect the mail, so I came back down. He was outside and noticed me. What are you doing here?"

"I was working the concert and spotted you a couple of hours ago. He's been harassing you since then?"

She shook her head. "No. I had to go back out a little while ago. Samantha, the girl I'm staying with, isn't feeling well. She asked me to pick up some cold medicine."

"I see. Are you hurt? He looked capable of anything."

"No. Thankfully, he was all hot air. He recognized

me from the news, though, and that set him off on another tirade. Thanks for coming to my rescue. Again. And don't tell me anyone would have intervened on my behalf, because too many people walked past us tonight ignoring me."

"I'm sorry. That's not right."

"Right or wrong, it is what it is. I feel like I should buy you a cup of coffee or something."

He shook his head. "Just stay out of trouble." He pulled out his new business card and handed it to her.

"What's this?"

"My business card. Keep it in case of an emergency."

Jenna read the card then tucked it into her jeans pocket. "Thanks. I appreciate this more than you know. The other day I thought for sure I heard someone following me to the bus stop, but when I looked, I didn't see anyone. It really creeped me out."

He blew out a breath. Unease settled on him. "If that happens again, get inside a safe place and call someone. You shouldn't be out alone at night either, considering you received a death threat."

Her face blanched.

He rested a hand on her shoulder and lowered his face to look into her eyes. "You're not going to pass out, are you?"

"No. But hearing you talk about that e-mail so bluntly…" She shivered. "I should go. Thanks for the help."

"Anytime. Good night, Jenna." He walked out the door. Fate had brought them together again. Was he making a mistake walking away a second time? He looked over his shoulder. She stood at the elevator door, her back to him. He believed in God not fate, and if He wanted their paths to cross again, they would with or without him getting her number. Besides, she knew how to reach him.

5

Carissa sat in a comfy lawn chair beside Marc on her apartment balcony that faced Lake Washington off in the distance. "I know we were working last night, but I enjoyed that concert."

"Not me. Way too loud."

"That's what earplugs are for."

He chuckled. "We finally have a couple of days off. What do you want to do today?"

"I don't know. Sitting here and relaxing with a good book sounds luxurious."

"We aren't an old married couple." He leaned forward, resting his elbows on his knees and tilting his head to face her. "Let's *do* something. We could go to the Boeing Space Museum, Pike Place Market, or rent kayaks or paddleboats at one of the lakes."

"Kayaking sounds like fun." Her phone rang. She picked it up and frowned.

"What's wrong?"

"It's Hannah from Gently Brewed." She accepted

the call. "Hi, Hannah. What's up?"

"I need you." Fear filled the young woman's voice. "Willy found my home," she spoke softly into the phone, but the clink of dishes and voices could be heard in the background.

Carissa stood, put the phone on speaker, and motioned for Marc to follow her inside. "The guy writing a movie? The one I talked with at the coffee shop?"

"That's him. Someone spray-painted an obscene message on the garage door of the home where I'm living. I didn't see him do it, but it had to be Willy. I can't imagine who else would have done it."

Had the screenwriter played her? Carissa's gut clenched. "Text me your address. I'll be there as soon as I can. Are you in a safe place?"

"I'm not sure a safe place exists. I left my home and came to the coffee shop. I was so scared I didn't know where else to go. The woman I live with is away until Monday."

"Okay. Sit tight. My associate and I will be there ASAP." She disconnected the call then turned to Marc. "Rain check on playing tourist?"

"Of course." He frowned. "You think Willy's the one who vandalized Hannah's house?"

"Hannah thinks so. It makes the most sense, but to be honest, it surprises me. He seemed legit."

Marc sighed. "So much for a relaxing weekend." He pulled his keys from his pocket. "Want me to drive?"

"No. I'll meet you there. We might need to split up. Be right back." She strode to her bedroom and removed the Glock from the lockbox on her nightstand then met Marc in the entryway. "See you there."

She slipped behind the wheel of her car and headed for the main road. Her phone rang again. She pressed the button on the steering wheel. "This is Carissa."

"He's here," Hannah said, her voice rising.

Hannah's frantic voice set off alarms in Carissa's mind. "Who's there?"

"Willy."

Carissa pressed the accelerator harder, signaled, and weaved through traffic. "Take a breath, Hannah."

She waited for the younger woman to do so. "Feel better?"

"A little. How much longer until you get here?"

"I'm about ten minutes away. What's he doing?" Carissa tightened her fingers around the steering wheel.

"He's sitting in his usual spot with his laptop."

"Has he threatened you in any way?" Carissa's pulse thrummed. She took her own advice and breathed in a deep breath.

"Not in so many words. But he's here!" She hissed into the phone.

"Okay. Are you working?" Carissa kept her voice calm and soothing.

"No. I'm just sitting here with a cup of tea."

"Do you think he followed you there?" The chances Hannah would have noticed being followed were slim, considering how upset she was.

"I don't know. Maybe. No. I was here at least five minutes before he walked in."

"Okay. Sit tight. Does anyone at the shop know what's going on?"

"Yes. I told my supervisor. He said I could sit here as long as I needed to."

"Good. Do you want me to stay on the phone with you until I get there?" She'd happily keep talking if it would help calm Hannah.

"No. You shouldn't talk on the phone and drive." The phone went silent.

Carissa slowed for a red light. "Call Marc." Her car connected her.

"What's up?"

"Willy's at the shop."

"I'm calling the police."

"We can't prove he did anything. At least not yet." The light changed. She punched the accelerator, and her car charged forward.

"She feels threatened and something happened at her home. The guy was told to stay away. Isn't that enough?" Frustration laced Marc's voice.

"Guess we'll find out. Go ahead and call." She pressed end and kept driving. Another five minutes, and they'd be there. Marc followed close behind her. Maybe the police would beat them to the scene if they were nearby. She ought to warn Hannah but didn't want to freak her out any more than she already was.

Miracle of miracles, traffic cleared, and they made it there in record time. She parked then strode inside. Hannah sat near the counter. Willy sat in his usual spot. A male stood at the register—must be the supervisor.

Carissa slid into the chair beside Hannah. "What happened? Tell me everything no matter how minor it might seem."

Hannah nodded and folding her shaking hands, rested them on the table.

"Before you begin, my associate felt it prudent to call the police. They'll be here any minute."

Tears formed in Hannah's eyes, and she nodded. "Okay. I'm so scared, Carissa."

Carissa rubbed her hand up and down Hannah's arm. "I understand. What happened?"

"When I went outside this morning to collect the paper, the garage door had been graffitied."

"What did it say?"

She shook her head. "It was b-bad. I c-can't."

"What makes you think it was directed at you?"

A male police officer Carissa didn't know walked in at that moment with Marc. They approached the women. "Ma'am, a call was placed on your behalf. Marc filled me in on what's been going on, but I'd like to hear it from you."

Hannah glanced toward Willy, who rushed to pack up. "He's going to get away. You have to stop him." She quickly repeated what she'd told Carissa a moment ago.

"Do you have any evidence to prove that man is the same person who vandalized your home?"

"Well, no. Not yet. I'm sure at least a few of the neighbors have security cameras mounted on their homes though. Can't you hold him on suspicion?"

"I'll talk to him." The officer turned to where Willy had been sitting.

Carissa's gaze swiveled to the door. "There." She pointed and stood. "He's going to get away."

The officer rushed after the man Hannah was concerned about. He stopped him right outside the door. A moment later, Willy took off running.

Carissa shook her head. "That was dumb." He had made his life so much more difficult than necessary. Carissa had hated foot chases when she was a cop. "Let's go back to your place, Hannah. I'd like to see the damage and talk to your neighbors. See if they saw anything or captured anything on their security cameras."

Marc shook the hand of the female homeowner across the street from Hannah's place. "Thanks for allowing me to view your security footage."

"No problem. I hope the cops catch the creep who did that." The woman shook her head, her lips skewed with disgust.

He pulled out his business card. "If you notice

anything suspicious or concerning, I'd appreciate a call."

"Sure. It makes me angry to think that someone is targeting Hannah. She's such a sweet girl. She's a full-time college student, working thirty hours a week, and still stops by just to be friendly. She even offered to walk my dog once when I wasn't feeling well."

"We all want her to be safe. Thanks again." He turned and headed across the street to where Carissa and Hannah stood talking with a man. Marc strolled over to the small group.

Carissa caught his eye and shook her head slightly. She wrapped up the conversation, and the man walked away.

Marc moved into their half circle. "Who was that?"

"A detective with the police department. Turns out the man you were concerned about isn't the perpetrator."

"I was going to tell you the same thing. The security camera across the street captured a good image of a woman."

Hannah frowned. "I can't believe a woman did this."

"Have you made anyone angry recently? Perhaps you went out with someone's boyfriend or husband?"

"No. I don't have time to date. My life is basically work and school. I'm supposed to be at the school right now for a study group." She worried her bottom lip.

Carissa pulled out a notepad from her pocket along with a mini pen. "Is there anyone in the group who might be angry with you?"

"I can't imagine why." She caught Marc's eye with her gaze. "I watched the footage you sent to my phone. I don't know who she is. Maybe she goes to the coffee shop, or she's in one of my classes. I honestly have no idea." She raised her hands in a shrug. "None of this makes sense. I thought for sure Willy was responsible."

"Any news on why he came back to the shop?" he addressed Carissa.

"He told the officer the other shop he'd planned to go to was closed."

"Then why run?"

"Apparently, when he asked for identification, Willy got spooked because he has several outstanding parking tickets."

Marc rubbed the back of his neck. "Okay. So much for a slam-dunk. Hannah, I think you should go to your study group. Show them the video and see if anyone recognizes the woman. One of us can accompany you if that would make you feel better."

Hannah squared her shoulders. "Thank you, but I need to be able to do this on my own. As it turns out, I can't afford a bodyguard."

He glanced at Carissa, hoping they were of the same mind.

She nodded.

"We have the weekend free to spend however we want. How about if we watch your back and maybe find this woman?"

"You'd do that for me?" Wonder filled Hannah's voice.

"You're Carissa's favorite barista, and in case you haven't noticed, she takes her coffee very seriously. Consider it self-preservation."

Wide-eyed, Hannah nodded. "I had no idea. Thank you. Both of you. Guess I'd better get a move on before my study group leaves."

They'd left Carissa's car at the coffee shop so she joined him in his pickup. "You are full of surprises."

"What? Did I make the wrong call?"

"No, but I thought you wanted to spend our rare weekend off playing tourist."

He shrugged. "What can I say? I don't like it when someone threatens a nice girl. From what I've heard, Hannah is worth the sacrifice."

Carissa's eyes widened. "Should I be jealous?"

He laughed. "No."

"Good." She pointed to a white economy-sized car that pulled off from a side street and rode Hannah's bumper. "Think that's the woman who left her mark on the house or simply a bad driver."

"Don't know, but I'm guessing bad driver." One thing was certain—this promised to be a long weekend. "Let's go. We don't want to lose her."

6

Monday evening at the start of her second week staying with Samantha, Jenna stared in disbelief at a small stack of notes addressed to her on plain white paper. "Why didn't anyone tell me about these sooner?"

Horror filled her. She was in big trouble. Heat consumed her. She fanned her face with the stack as she paced in front of Samantha's living room couch. The words *Traitor* and *Liar* from the creepy notes seared in her mind.

Samantha shifted in her seat at her kitchen table. "Josh thought it would be best for the company to keep it quiet."

"It's my life on the line, and all he considered was Ads by Design?" Maybe getting fired had been a blessing rather than a curse. She didn't want someone like that as a boss. She wanted someone who cared—someone like Suzie or even that other lady. What was her name? Brandi something. She still had her card in her purse. Maybe she'd give her a call after all. Part-time work was better than no work.

"What are you going to do?"

"Call my dad. And before you say it, I'm not being a princess. You'd call yours too if something like this happened to you." She waved the stack of papers with notes on them pieced together from cut out letters and glued to printer paper. "Where were these found?"

"Every day for the past week one was slid under the front door."

"You knew about the death threat I had on my last day, and you didn't think I needed to know about these?" She didn't care if she sounded hysterical or if the neighbors heard. "How could you not tell me?"

"I'm telling you now, but you can't go to the police. I might get fired. Josh's order was implicit. No one was to breathe a word about the letters. He was afraid of more bad PR."

Jenna closed her eyes and fought to calm down and clear her racing thoughts. There had to be a way to find out who left the letters. Someone had to have noticed a person who didn't belong there. Her eyes flew open. "Ads by Design has a security camera at the entrance. Surely, the person can be identified." Odd, though, that the notes started arriving after she'd been fired. Clearly, the person who left them didn't know her status of employment.

Samantha shook her head. "Sorry. He must know about the camera because he always keeps his face turned away. It looks like he's wearing padding, so it's difficult to get a fix on his size."

"Figures. Well, thanks for giving these to me."

"Of course. I'm sorry for not doing so sooner." Her face softened. "What are you going to do?

"For starters, call my dad." Jenna made the call and explained the situation.

"Have you gone to the police?" Dad asked.

"I can't. Samantha might lose her job. She stole the evidence from Josh's office after being told he didn't want anyone to say anything."

"Of all the rotten, no-good things to do. Doesn't he have a clue what could happen due to his negligence?"

"I don't think he cares. What should I do?"

"A man at our church runs a security firm. I'll give him a call and set up a meeting. Maybe he can help."

"How much will that cost?"

"Don't worry about the money. If you can't pay the bill, your mom and I will help, and you can pay us back when you're able."

"Okay." Her entire body shook. "I've been working hard to pay down my student loans, but I still have some savings."

"Don't worry, Princess. I'll call him right now."

"Thanks." She ended the call and stood. She needed to do something, but what? She thought about Peter King. He worked at a place that protected people. Maybe she should call him. No. Dad was on top of the situation.

Samantha stood and poured them each a glass of water. "My mom used to always give me water when I was hurt. I know this isn't the same thing, but maybe it'll help."

Jenna took the glass. "Thanks." She moved over to the couch and sank onto it. "I need a distraction. Tell me about your mom."

Samantha sat beside her. "Let's see. She's a nurse and loves to ride motorcycles."

Jenna's eyes widened. "That's an interesting hobby for a nurse."

"Yeah. She's something."

"Just like her daughter. I think you might be the best friend I've ever had. You took me in when I was at my lowest, and you were the only person who cared enough to let me know about the notes." She hugged her friend. "Thank you."

Samantha's gaze shifted away and rested on Tinker, who hopped into her lap. She ran her fingers through Tinker's fur. "You're welcome. You might have been stupid by saying things you shouldn't have, but you don't deserve this. No one does." Samantha's words, though meant to be supportive, stung.

Her phone rang. "Hey, Dad." She stood and walked to the opposite end of the small room.

"Hi, Princess. You have an appointment tomorrow afternoon at two. Do you have a pencil to write down the address?"

"Go ahead." She typed the address into her phone. "Thanks, Dad. Will you be there too?"

"I can't. Prior commitment."

"Okay. How did things go with the board members?"

"We can talk about that later. First, let's make sure you're safe."

"But—"

"No buts. I don't want you worrying about me. Take care of yourself. Frank is a good man and has a great team working for him. Listen to what he says. I trust him."

Weariness settled on her. "I will. Thanks for setting this up. I'll be there."

"Let me know how it goes. Love you."

"Love you too." She ended the call and looked around Samantha's apartment. She needed to get out of here. It was too small for two people, and she'd over-stayed her welcome. First thing tomorrow, she would call Brandi about the job and start apartment hunting.

A dish shattered in the kitchen about five feet away. "Are you okay?"

"Yes, but my favorite ice cream dish isn't." Samantha bent over and swept the glass into a dustpan. "This has been the worst day."

"I'm really sorry about your day, but maybe this will brighten it for you. I'm going to follow up on a job lead in the morning and go apartment hunting."

"You don't have to rush, but to be honest, I appreciate that you are moving on. We both know this situation can't work forever. It's too tight in here." Samantha stood and dumped the contents of the dustpan into the trashcan.

"That's for sure. I hope you don't feel like I took advantage. I really thought I'd find another job, and life would go on."

"Life has gone on, just not the way you'd planned."

"Yeah," Jenna said softly. She took a breath and blew it out between her lips.

"The company's been nice." Samantha's lips twitched. "Most of the time."

"Thanks, I appreciate that. I'm looking forward to sleeping in a bed again." As comfortable as Samantha's couch was, she needed her own space.

"When do you think you'll be out? I'm not pushing, just curious."

Jenna made a quick decision. The sooner she left the better. "Tonight. After seeing those letters, I want to go home to be with my parents."

Relief shone on Samantha's face. It looked like she was more than a little happy to be rid of Jenna.

Jenna frowned. There was no way those letters were only a bad joke, which made her wonder about the e-mail. Were they connected? "I'll be out of here as soon as I can get a car to pick me up." She opened the ride share app on her phone and ordered a pick up. She had ten minutes—just enough time to gather her stuff.

She should probably call Mom and Dad and let them know she was headed home, but surprising them would be more fun.

Forty minutes later, suitcase by her side, Jenna stood at the door of her childhood home. She raised her hand to knock since she felt funny about going in unannounced. Raised voices made her pause. Her parents were shouting at each other. She gasped. They never fought. She put her ear to the door. They were arguing about *her*. She gasped, and her stomach knotted.

"If you wouldn't give in to Jenna's every wish and force her to be an adult, we wouldn't be in this situation," Mom shouted. "You're too easy on her."

Mom thought Dad was babying her. As if. For the first time in her life, he was doing exactly the opposite. Coming home had been a bad idea. She couldn't go back to Samantha's place though. She turned, gazing at her old neighborhood. She'd thought coming home would make everything feel okay again, but she was wrong. She felt worse than ever. Now where would she go?

She'd had a playhouse in the backyard growing up—it was more of a shed, but she'd loved it regardless. The last time she saw it, it still appeared well cared for. Maybe Mom had kept the inside fresh and clean too. As a child she'd often fallen asleep on the loveseat while reading. Staying there for one night wouldn't be so bad, even without power.

She skittered around the house and crept through the gate leading to the huge backyard she'd loved as a child. She paused, allowing her eyes to adjust to the ever-increasing darkness. At least there were decorative lights on the patio, so she could see somewhat.

She moved gingerly from one stone to the next on the pathway to her playhouse then opened the door.

Too bad there wasn't a light. She pulled out her phone and tapped the flashlight app illuminating the small space. Everything was pretty much as it had been when she was a kid except for the addition of an easel and a table covered in paints and other supplies.

Her mom loved to paint. She must have moved her studio out here. At least the loveseat was still here. She closed the door, set her suitcase down, then curled up on the only piece of padded furniture in the small space. This would do for tonight, but tomorrow she'd have to find a hotel room.

Sally tapped the corner of Peter's desk at Protection Inc. "Frank has a new client in his office. He wants us in there."

Peter stood. He'd taken a late lunch and missed seeing the client arrive. "What do you know?"

"She's the daughter of Frank's pastor. Oh, and Marc and Clarissa are on another case. I don't expect we'll be seeing much of them until the woman they're protecting either discharges them or her stalker is found."

"Hmm." That explained why they weren't in the office yesterday.

"Exactly." Her brow furrowed. Did she think they wouldn't be able to handle things without Marc and Carissa?

They walked across the sparse, bullpen-like space to Frank's office, went in without knocking, and stood along the back wall. The room lacked the niceties one would expect in a boss's office. But the basics were there—a metal desk, a file cabinet, and two wood chairs with padded leather seats for clients.

Frank nodded to them. "I'd like to introduce Jenna Walsh."

Jenna turned in her seat. Her eyes widened when her gaze landed on Peter. "This is where you work?"

Frank looked between him and Jenna. "I take it you know each other?"

"We've met," Peter said. "This is the woman I told you about." What kind of trouble was she in this time?

"You told Frank about me?" Her face registered shock.

"I was concerned for you. Sounds like with good reason since you're now here."

Frank fanned the letters out across his desk to face them.

The one closest read: *You ruined everything. Now you pay.*

"It appears as though someone isn't very happy with you, Miss Walsh." Frank looked up from the letters.

"Call me Jenna, please. I think there're a lot of someone's not happy with me, but this person took it too far. What should I do?"

"We can offer you advice on staying vigilant about

your surroundings and teach you some basic self-defense. We can also try and locate the person sending you these notes." Frank's gaze locked on Jenna's. "You should know these people mean business. Not to scare you any more than you are already, but your video ignited a firestorm for the chairman of the board at Kratt Paper. Someone tried to kill him over it."

Jenna gasped. "I never meant for any of this to happen. Me and my stupid temper. Is Mr. Wood okay?"

"You know Mr. Wood?" Frank asked.

"Of course, I'm quite familiar with everyone on their board. I worked closely with several of those backstabbers." She shook her head. "Sorry. I'm trying to guard my tongue better. I shouldn't have said that."

Peter stuck a thumb through one of the belt loops on his jeans as things he'd been observing since starting work at Protection Inc. started to make sense. Apparently, they did more than protect people—they did detective work as well. He probably should have figured that out already since Sally did much of her work on the computer. Now he knew what she'd been doing—investigating. It all made sense now.

"Do you think I need protection?" Fear filled Jenna's voice.

Frank had filled in Peter about the particulars of the now closed Wood case, but Peter didn't want to believe Jenna's situation was connected. The idea was unsettling to say the least. Her problem was even more complicated than he'd suspected. He'd been concerned about Jenna's e-mail before, but this new development set him on edge.

He wanted to tell her she'd be fine and to ignore the notes, but when someone took the time to cut out little letters from multiple sources to create a threatening message, there was no telling what they were capable of doing. That, in addition to the e-mail, made brushing this off as a joke impossible. "Where're you living? Are you still staying with your friend?" Peter asked.

"I'm between places right now." Her face turned a pretty shade of pink.

"You're homeless?" Sally clarified.

"Sort of, but not exactly."

Frank frowned. "Your dad didn't mention this when we spoke yesterday."

"He doesn't know. I was staying on a former co-worker's couch until last night when I learned about this." She motioned toward the letters. "At that point, I decided leaving would be best."

Sally wrinkled her nose. "With no place to go?"

"I thought I had a place, but it…didn't work out. I'll get a hotel room until I can find a new apartment."

If her parents were in the area why wouldn't she go there? This didn't make sense. Clearly there was more to the story.

"I apologize if we seem intrusive with our questions," Frank said, "but the more we know about your situation the better we can advise and help you."

"I understand." Jenna fiddled with the hem of her blouse. "I followed up on a job lead this morning and hope to hear back about it soon. Once I know if it's going to work out, I'll apply at an apartment near the office since I don't have a car."

"No car?" Sally narrowed her eyes. "I'm missing something. Your outfit probably cost three hundred dollars, yet you're homeless, jobless, and without a car. What happened?"

"I made a mistake that cost me everything," Jenna said softly.

Peter's heart hurt for Jenna. "The complex I moved into has a vacancy. It's only a single bedroom apartment on the south side of Seattle." What was he doing? He didn't want or need this woman as his next-door neighbor.

"So is my job lead. Thanks for the tip. It's tough to find one-bedroom apartment openings."

He'd considered the smaller unit for himself, but the two-bedroom apartment had a better layout and wasn't much more money. He pulled a pen from his jacket pocket and tore a piece of paper from the notepad he carried—a habit born from his days as a cop. Then he wrote the name of the complex along with the address. "It's nothing fancy, but it's in a safe neighborhood, and it's well tended."

She took the slip of paper. "Thanks."

Frank cleared his throat. "How about you let Sally teach you a few evasive maneuvers before you leave. I'll be in touch with a plan of action."

"Okay. How much will all this cost?"

Frank tossed out a number that seemed quite reasonable.

She didn't give her thoughts away when she nodded and stood. "You'll call when you find this person?"

"Absolutely. Your dad said your former co-worker took these from her place of employment, and that's why you won't go to the police. I think you'd be wise to let them know what's going on regardless."

"I don't want to get her fired. She took me in when I was at my lowest."

Frank nodded. "I understand."

"Jenna," Peter said. "Do you still have that e-mail you received the day you were let go?"

She nodded.

"Will you forward it to Frank right now?"

"Sure." She pulled out her phone. "Do you really think they're from the same person?"

"I don't know."

Frank tapped his keyboard keys. "Got it. Thanks."

Sally and Jenna left the room.

Peter raised a brow. "What do you think?"

"I'm not sure. Everything about this case is odd. There are no demands and no clear threat." He looked at the computer screen and sucked in a sharp breath. "I take it back. Why didn't she get help after receiving this e-mail?"

"I suggested she contact the police, but she believed

it was intended as a joke. Shortly after the e-mail arrived, she was let go from her job. Can we trace the sender?"

Frank tapped keys again. "It's probably a dummy account, but I'll work on it. For now, what's your take on the notes? Why leave them after she was fired?"

"Excellent question. Maybe whoever left them doesn't realize she was let go?"

Frank rested his elbow on his desk. "Going with that theory, who do you like for this?"

"Too soon to say. I need more information." He had yet come up with who he thought was behind this. "I'm not convinced it's not someone from her office. They could have been leaving the notes there to throw everyone off."

"Possibly. What clues can we get from the notes?"

"You pay. Could be in reference to losing her job. The notes might have been taunting her rather than threatening, but it's difficult to know for sure. One thing is certain, if they were only trying to scare her. I'd say they succeeded."

Frank leaned back in his chair. "I remember you talked with me about her, but there seems to be more to the story."

"There's no story. Like I said, we met at our mutual storage unit facility. A tower of boxes fell on her. Then I rescued her. The night of the concert in the park I spotted her having a confrontation with a man. I stepped in, and that's when I gave her my card."

Frank rubbed his chin and had an unfocused gaze. "In context, those boxes falling make me think twice." He angled his head toward Peter. "You said she wasn't hurt right?"

"Minor cut. Why?"

"It makes me wonder if the incident wasn't an accident. What do you think?" Frank studied his face.

"Accident. No doubt. They were precariously stacked."

"You saw them before they fell?" He raised a brow.

"Yes." His boss didn't need the specifics of their first meeting.

"Okay. I'll follow up with my buddy at the PD. See if they have any cases like ours."

Peter nodded and stood. "Do you need anything further from me right now?"

"Keep eyes on Jenna. Until we know what we're dealing with, I'd feel better knowing she's safe."

"Yes, sir."

"Sally will relieve you later. For now, I need her here doing some research on Miss Walsh. Marc and Carissa are tied up on another job so you're on your own for a bit. I'll be in touch with details." He nodded toward the window that faced the bullpen. "Looks like they're done with the self-defense lesson. You better get a move on."

"We could ask to track her phone." He didn't want to lose her, and in a city this big, that was a distinct possibility.

"Good idea but still keep an eye on her. If anyone tries anything, I want you there to stop them."

"Will do." Tracking her phone wouldn't give her the protection detail his boss clearly wanted her to have, but the price he'd quoted didn't come close to covering that kind of job. He must think a lot of her dad.

Peter walked into the bullpen. "Can I give you a ride somewhere, Jenna? I'm on my way out." Playing taxi would be much simpler than following her all over the city.

A blank look covered her face.

"You do have somewhere to go, don't you?"

"Umm." She pulled out her phone and looked at the screen. "I'm in limbo until I hear back about the job."

"Is that your only lead?"

She nodded. "Where are you headed?"

Wherever you are. This was not working out like he'd expected. "How about coffee? There's a great little place a couple doors down."

"I thought you were driving somewhere." She frowned.

"Change of plans."

She studied his face for a moment as if trying to read his mind. "Sure, coffee sounds nice, but it's my treat—I owe you. Plus, I could use a pick-me-up after the night I had." She shivered.

There was definitely a story there. He held the door open. "After you."

"Thanks." She walked out then stopped, waiting for him. "Which way?"

He veered to the right. "What happened last night?"

"Why do you ask?"

"You alluded to a difficult night. Since you hired us, I thought it would be prudent to know if something happened that concerned you."

"Oh." Her gaze shifted away from his then back. "It was concerning, but not related to this."

Hmm. "Are you sure? The seemingly insignificant can sometimes be important."

"Unless me spending the night in my childhood playhouse on a dusty loveseat because I was too chicken to knock on my parents' front door is related to this, then please let it go."

He hadn't expected to hear that. So she had gone to her parents' place after all? This didn't make sense. Her dad was the one to contact Frank, so clearly, they had at least some kind of relationship. "Why were you afraid to knock?"

"So much for letting it go," she mumbled.

He chuckled. "Sorry. I have need-to-know disease."

She rolled her eyes. "I overheard a conversation that would have made my being there uncomfortable for everyone. It's a family thing."

"Okay. I'm sorry if I overstepped."

"It's fine."

But was it? Talking about her family appeared to have made her sad on top of everything else she was dealing with. All things considered, she was one strong lady.

He opened the door to his favorite coffee shop—well, it was the only one he'd seen that was close enough to walk to for a quick break. The rich scent of coffee enveloped him. The warm autumn colors on walls welcomed them in further. "What would you like?"

She pulled out her wallet. "My treat. Remember?"

"Right." They stepped up to the counter. "How's your afternoon, Rebecca?" he asked the blonde running the cash register.

"Not bad. I was wondering if you'd be in today. You're a little late."

"Been busy. I'll have a small black coffee and my friend would like…" He looked at Jenna.

"A medium iced coffee please." She handed over a ten-dollar bill.

Peter had only been on the job a few days, but Rebecca had been here every time he'd come in.

"Sure thing." Rebecca gave Jenna her change then poured his coffee. "Here you go. See you tomorrow?" A twinkle lit her eyes.

"It's possible. I almost always need a caffeine fix." He raised his cup to her. "Thanks." He turned to find Jenna watching them with interest. He walked with her to the other end of the counter where she waited for her drink.

"You have an admirer." She kept her voice low,

presumably to not embarrass Rebecca.

"You think so?" Had he read the twinkle in her eyes wrong? He'd thought she was simply a happy and friendly person. He glanced back at the young woman.

"Oh, I know so." Jenna nodded to the next customer in line. "Look how she's talking to that guy. See how she's not really looking at him?"

"Stop analyzing the poor girl." He glanced toward Rebecca. The sparkle she had had when she talked to him was missing. Maybe Jenna was right. He was flattered but not even remotely interested.

The barista slid a drink across the counter. "Here you go."

Jenna took her drink. "Thanks. Are we sitting or walking?" Her phone rang. She pulled it from her purse, and her face lit. "I need to take this. Do you mind if we sit in that corner?" She motioned to a table as far from the activity in the shop as possible.

He led the way.

"This is Jenna."

His interest piqued as he strained to listen to both sides of the conversation but only caught snippets of the woman's voice on the other end. It sounded like good news, though. He sat at the table in the seat facing the entrance. Jenna eased onto the chair across from him.

"I can start first thing tomorrow. Thank you, Brandi." She placed her phone on the tabletop. "I got the job." Her face glowed with happiness. "It's only part time and quite a step down from what I had before, but it's a job. Right now, that's what's most important. It's hard to get an apartment when you're unemployed."

"Congratulations. Does that mean we're going to be neighbors?" It would be a lot easier keeping an eye on her if they were.

"I need to call and see if the apartment is still available." She sipped her coffee for a moment then made the call.

He kept watch on the door and everyone who came and went. No one paid Jenna any special attention. He tasted his coffee. *Mmm.* As wonderful as the last cups he'd enjoyed.

Jenna pulled her phone away and looked at him expectantly. "Do you have time to run me over to the complex? If not, I can get a rideshare."

"Save your money. I'll take you."

"Thanks." She told the person on the other end she'd be right over then started tapping away at her phone.

"What are you doing?"

"Texting Brandi for a favor, and then I'm going to the apartment complex website to fill out the application."

"Don't you want to see the apartment first?"

"It's a few blocks from my new workplace, and I don't have a car. You vouched for it. That's good enough for me."

"Then why go see it?"

"I want the keys. By the time we get there, the application should have gone through. Brandi said she'd fax over a copy of my proof of employment. With that and my excellent credit rating, it should go through fast." She stood, still tapping at the phone screen. "You ready?"

"Sure." She was making his job very easy, but he knew better than to become complacent. Anything could happen at any moment, and he needed to be ready.

7

Marc stepped out of the kitchen into the dining area of the coffee shop after Peter and a woman left. He'd seen Peter approaching from the live security feed in the manager's office and chose to stay out of sight.

News that Hannah lived in the home of a federal judge had changed everything. They were now officially working Hannah's protection detail, and he was at Gently Brewed to make sure their security was adequate.

Judge Alyssa Potter had the U.S. Marshals watching her back, and the FBI was following up on the evidence. Until further notice, they were looking out for the judge's pet project—Hannah Combs. Meanwhile, Carissa and Hannah were attending Hannah's classes at the University of Washington.

A commotion near the door drew his attention. He glanced toward Rebecca who stood behind the counter taking an order. Her panicked gaze met his.

"Watch where you're going." The shorter of two men pushed the other one.

What is this, the kindergarten playground? Marc strode to the men who, by the look of it, had collided and caused one of them to drop his drink. "Excuse me. Is there anything I can do to help?"

Angry eyes slammed into his. "This bozo wasn't watching where he was going and made me spill my drink."

Marc met the gaze of the other man who pulled out his wallet and tossed the shorter guy a twenty. "That should cover your drink and cleaning bill." He walked out without a backward glance.

The man with the stained shirt snagged the twenty and stuffed it in his pocket then left without reordering his drink. The guy had probably caused the accident on purpose to con the man into giving him money. Marc shook his head. He shouldn't be so cynical.

Rebecca stood behind the counter open-mouthed then snapped her lips together.

"Are you okay?" Marc asked.

Rebecca nodded. "Yes. I'm sure glad you were here. Thank you for dealing with those men. We don't normally have people behaving like that in here— especially businessmen. I hate confrontation."

"I think most of us do."

"Yeah. I suppose you're right. Thanks again." She slipped off her apron before disappearing into the back room. Several minutes later she emerged wearing an outfit straight out of the twenties.

"Are you headed to a party in the middle of the afternoon?"

She chuckled. "I have an audition."

"You act?" This was news.

"Any chance I get. See you. Amy's in back. She'll be right out to take my place." She waved and strode away.

Carissa escorted Hannah into Gently Brewed. Marc sat at a corner table, looking worse for the wear. Concern filled her. Had something happened? Surely, he would have sent a message.

Hannah waved to a customer who said hi to her then turned to Carissa. "Thanks for dropping me off. Will you be staying?"

"Yes. I'm your sidekick until something changes." Even though the feds thought the judge was the target, Carissa couldn't shake the feeling Hannah was the one in danger. Their involvement meant she could focus on keeping her client safe while the FBI searched for the perpetrator.

She slid onto the seat beside Marc's. "How's it going? You look bothered."

"The surveillance camera is in good working order. Anyone coming in or out of the front door is recorded, and the stream is stored in a cloud."

She nodded. "What else is going on?"

"Two guys got into it a little bit ago. Guess I let it get to me." He rubbed his chin. "I can't help but wonder if either of them is connected in any way to our case. One of them has serious anger issues."

"But Hannah wasn't even here. Besides that, the surveillance clearly showed a woman spray painting the garage door."

"Which is why I'm perplexed. Rebecca made me think of another idea."

"The barista?"

"Yes. She's an actress. With the right stuff anyone could look like anyone they wish. What if the *woman* we saw wasn't really a woman but a man?"

Carissa sucked in a breath. It wouldn't change how they did their job, but would it change the scope of the FBI's investigation? Surely, they were on top of that possibility already. "Interesting thought. Did you tell Frank?"

He shook his head. "He's swamped. He accepted a case from a friend on top of the normal workload."

She wrinkled her nose. "And we took on Hannah without a second thought to how busy everyone already is. I understand how he couldn't turn away this unexpected client. How's he doing?"

"You know Frank. He's always okay. Somehow everyone will get the service they paid for, even if that means we work without much sleep."

"Good thing we hired Peter. By the way, what do you think of him?"

"So far I like him. He has a good eye for trouble and proved himself at the concert last Friday."

"I agree." She stood. "I'm going to get a drink.

Would you like water?"

"That sounds great. Much better than the vile stuff you drink."

She wrinkled her nose at him then headed for the counter where Hannah now worked. "Could I get a chai latte and a cup of water please?"

"Sure thing. My boss said to give you both anything you want."

"That's not necessary." She pulled out her wallet.

"I can't take your money, Carissa."

She blew out a breath. "Fine. Please thank your boss. When you get a break, I have some questions about your relationship to the judge."

Hannah's hand hovered over a stack of paper cups. "I don't know what you're talking about. We don't have a relationship other than she's my landlord."

Carissa narrowed her eyes. Why would her client lie to her? "You might want to rethink my services if you can't trust me." There was no way a federal judge would house a random college student. There had to be more to the story, and she was determined to learn the truth. She moved to the other end of the counter where their drinks would be served.

Hannah scooted her direction. "I signed a non-disclosure agreement," she said barely above a whisper. "I can't talk about anything that I might overhear or see at Alyssa's."

Alyssa? She called the judge by her first name? Then again, that probably wasn't all that odd for someone living in her home. But an NDA? Now that was odd. This case just became a lot more intriguing. Carissa collected their drinks then joined Marc. "I learned something very interesting." She leaned close and repeated what Hannah had said.

Marc frowned and sat back, shifting his gaze to their client. "Hmm."

"What?" Carissa asked.

"I think we should have a talk with the judge."

Carissa grinned. "I like how your brain works. We already have clearance to be at the house." Now to wait for Hannah's shift to end so they could quiz her hostess.

8

Marc stood beside the window in Judge Potter's house. Carissa and Hannah sat on a stuffy looking sofa. Hannah appeared ready to collapse. He could use some shuteye too. But until the judge arrived with her protection detail they were stuck.

A black sedan pulled along the curb and parked in front of the house then another parked in the driveway. The judge had finally made it home. Did she always get home after seven or was today special?

A U.S. Marshal opened her door. Then they strode to the house together. The judge's blue eyes lit when they landed on Hannah. "You're home. Don't you normally have evening activities?"

"Not tonight. I wanted to give Carissa and Marc a break, so I came home."

The judge suddenly seemed weary as she addressed Carissa. "Thank you for seeing her safely home. You can take off now."

Carissa stood. "We were hoping to talk with you in

private." She glanced toward the marshal who had accompanied the judge inside. "If that's all right?"

"It's up to the judge," the marshal said.

"We can talk in the kitchen. I'm starving." Judge Potter headed toward a chef's dream kitchen—stainless steel fridge, gas cooktop, double oven, and white quartz counters atop navy blue cabinets. She pulled open the fridge and took out a salad and a platter of something. "My cook comes by in the morning and leaves dinner for Hannah and me." She opened the microwave and placed the platter inside. "What is it you need to speak with me about?"

Carissa gave Marc's arm a squeeze as if to say I've got this. "As you know, my associate and I are not convinced the message left on your garage was intended for you. Not long before that vandalism happened, Hannah had contacted me regarding her personal safety. She felt as though she was being stalked by someone who frequented Gently Brewed."

The judge stilled. "Go on. Hannah hasn't told me this."

"I don't think she wanted to burden you with her problem. Anyway, it appeared to be a false alarm, but now we aren't certain it was. We're curious why a successful woman such as yourself would allow a college student to stay in your home. Hannah claims you have no relationship outside of you being her landlord, but it's something I'm having a hard time accepting. On top of that, a non-disclosure agreement for a student living in your home seems over the top."

The judge's gaze locked on Carissa's. "One might think so until they've had trusted house staff betray their confidence. It's something anyone who spends time in my home must sign."

Carissa held her steely gaze. "I see. I take it someone tried to ruin you?"

"She did and thankfully failed. My NDA policy was adopted after that. As for why I would allow Hannah to live here, let's say I have a soft spot for college students. I set up a scholarship at the local university with the hope of giving back and making a difference in the life of an outstanding student."

"You became altruistic somewhat recently. According to my research, this is the first year the scholarship was offered. Why?" Carissa asked.

"You're a bold woman, Miss Jones. To come into my home and question me like this takes moxie. I respect that." She broke eye contact. "Maybe you should have gone into law."

Carissa let out the breath. "Thank you. I was a cop for a while, but I realize that's not what you meant. Back to my question. Why the sudden generosity?"

The judge pulled open a drawer. "Everything has a beginning." She waved a spoon in the air. "It's been a long day. I'm hungry and tired. Unless you have something more, I would like for you to leave."

Marc stepped forward. "Thank you for your time. We'll be digging into Hannah's life, trying to figure out who's behind her trouble. Are you sure you don't have anything you'd like to tell us?"

"I can't imagine what. We are nothing more than landlord and tenant."

And I'm Bugs Bunny. He didn't know what their connection was, but there was definitely something other than the obvious. Based on the fact that the judge and Hannah shared the same eye shape and color, he suspected they were, at least, related.

"Does she know she's your daughter?" Carissa asked.

Judge Potter stilled. "This conversation is over. I suggest you keep that speculation to yourself, Miss Jones." She directed them to the front door. "I believe you know your way out."

Once outside, Marc blew a long low whistle. "Lady, you have—"

"Don't say moxie." She glanced at him as they headed for his pickup. They'd left her vehicle at the coffee shop.

"I can't believe you said that."

Carissa opened the door to his pickup and hopped in. "It popped out."

Marc settled behind the wheel and turned over the engine. He pulled out and headed back to the coffee shop. "What makes you think Judge Potter is Hannah's mother?"

"The eyes."

"I noticed their eyes too, but she could as easily be

her aunt or cousin or some distant relative." He signaled and turned the corner.

"I didn't think of that. She's the right age to be Hannah's mom."

"Or aunt."

She huffed out a breath. "Fine. You know I don't normally blurt out what I'm thinking. I don't know why I said that. Her response seemed to indicate I could be right."

"To my way of thinking, the only thing it showed was annoyance with a nosey bodyguard who most, present company excluded, would say overstepped."

"You don't think I made a mistake revealing what I thought? I sure do."

"I didn't say that, but I don't think you overstepped. You have a legitimate concern for our client. If Hannah is her daughter, that changes things. It's something we need to know."

"Good luck finding out now. Rather than confront the judge, I should have asked my friend what she could find out for us. Confronting her like that lacked judgment and forethought."

He chuckled.

"What?"

"I don't think either of us considered the consequences. We're burning the candle at both ends and need to take a step back to think."

"Yeah," she said softly.

Normally, she would argue, but maybe she didn't have the energy. "You okay?" He reached for her hand.

"Just tired. I wonder if Sally's free."

"You thinking about stepping back?"

She nodded. "I realize Hannah isn't a ten-year-old, but she's barely eighteen and vulnerable. I'm not sure I have the emotional energy to take on another young person so soon after Olivia."

"Hannah is an adult. It's not the same."

"I know, but it sure feels that way. She is so innocent and naïve."

The little girl they'd protected this past summer had worn Carissa out emotionally. She probably should have taken more than a couple of weeks off before jumping back into the grind. He could say one thing for sure about his business partners—they were not lazy. Those two kept busier than a colony of ants.

He cleared his throat. "Maybe talking with a counselor will help."

She frowned and pulled her hand from his. "I'll manage."

Carissa had once shared with him that protecting young people reminded her of the day when she was ten and her mom was mugged. This wasn't the first time it had happened and probably wouldn't be the last. "I think bringing Sally in is a good idea. How about you give her a call and see if she's available tomorrow to attend classes with Hannah?"

Carissa shot off a text to Sally. A moment later her phone chimed a reply.

She read the text out loud. "Frank has me on another case. Everything okay?" Carissa frowned.

"You could always talk to Frank about a switch. He'd understand."

"I'd never hear the end of it. No, thanks. I'll tell Sally everything is fine and not to worry about it." Her thumbs flew across the keyboard on her phone's screen. Then she rested her head back and closed her eyes.

The sun had set long ago as Marc strode beside Frank on their way out of their office building. The lack of foot traffic testified to the late hour. A pickup in need of a new muffler rumbled past them. "I'm concerned for Carissa."

Frank slowed. "Why's that?"

"The case that Carissa and I took on this weekend is stirring up old memories for her."

"You mean like last summer's client did?"

"Afraid so. I suggested she see a counselor." He'd regretted the words from the moment they'd popped out of his mouth. Carissa had been withdrawn ever since. Granted that had been less than a day, but even a half of a day was too long to be on the outs with the love of his life. He hurt when she hurt, and he hated hurting.

Frank blew out a breath. "I imagine that didn't go well."

He shrugged. "Could've gone better." He tilted his head. "What do you make of Jenna? It's pretty crazy that we were already protecting someone else because of her."

Frank slowed. "Yeah. It certainly does make me wonder."

"'Bout what?"

"About who's behind the threats she received. We already know someone was willing to kill Jason over what she said on the video. Are we dealing with individuals out to cause trouble or a group willing to take matters into their own hands?"

"Yeah. I see where you're going. Makes you wonder how many others are being threatened too."

"Exactly. And all because of an anger-induced rant that some cruel person posted online." Frank stuffed a hand into his jeans pocket. "I have to get going. Do you and Carissa need additional support protecting Hannah?"

"I think we have her covered." As tempting as it was to ask Frank to pull Sally from her current client, he wouldn't. Carissa would have to make that call.

"With the marshals involved, I imagine the person behind the graffiti will be caught sooner rather than later." Frank pulled keys from his pocket.

"We can hope." Marc appreciated that the feds were involved, but they were focused on protecting the judge, not her tenant. "Have a good night." He'd swing by Carissa's before heading to his condo. One way or another, they were going to have a few minutes alone off the clock.

9

Jenna stood in the doorway of her new second level apartment, which happened to be right next to Peter's. "I can't thank you enough for helping me move all my stuff." A horn honked in the parking lot below. It would have been nice to live in a building with a doorman, like she used to, but there was something to be said for having easy access to outdoors—all she had to do was step out her front door.

"It was no problem, and I was happy to help." Peter glanced toward his place.

"I'll let you go. See you." She moved to close the door.

"Wait."

She paused. Her entire body hurt from carrying boxes, and all she wanted was a hot bath. Not that she could take one without scrubbing the tub first.

"Do you need a ride to go car shopping?"

"Thanks, but I'm not getting a car."

"Seriously?"

She understood his skepticism. Until a month ago, she'd avoided public transit. "I want to see how my new job goes before tying myself down to an auto loan."

He nodded, but his eyes held questions.

She sighed. "What is it? I know you want to ask something else."

He chuckled. "You read people well."

"It's one of the reasons I was so good at my job." Clearly, she'd misread someone, though.

"You stated before that your old job paid for your housing and car. With all that money you saved, I would think you'd have enough laying around to buy a car."

Her eyes widened. "I used the money I would have put into rent to pay down my student loans. So contrary to what it might look like, I'm not rich or hoarding a load of cash." She was too tired to be annoyed by his question. Forget the bath. Give her a pillow and blanket, and she'd be happy.

He nodded. "Got it. I apologize for assuming."

"Apology accepted. Thanks again." She closed her door. She didn't have much since her first apartment had come furnished, but she'd make do with sleeping on the floor tonight. She unpacked the necessities then boiled water for a Cup of Noodles.

She piled throw pillows into a corner and settled onto them with her dinner. Her thoughts drifted to Peter. He'd been a constant in her life since this afternoon. What a trooper. He'd winced a couple of times and placed his hand at the crook of his back to stretch as if his back pained him, but he hadn't complained once.

Her gaze landed on the box with her high school memories—tiara included. Senior year had been epic. She'd not only been prom queen but homecoming queen as well. Had she peaked in high school? She shook off the ridiculous thought. No way had that been as good as it got. Her career had been amazing and could be again—no *would* be again. She only needed to keep her temper in check and her opinions to herself.

Brandi seemed like she'd be a fair boss and already had a project for her. She couldn't wait to start work tomorrow. Too bad it was only part time, but maybe she could take on some graphic art jobs online. She'd need to bring in more income soon, or she'd be eating a Cup of Noodles every night.

Her phone rang. She reached for it—Dad. "Hey, there."

"How'd it go with Frank?"

"He's looking into the situation." Unease crept over her. She'd been so busy today she'd avoided thinking about those creepy notes. "I didn't realize they did detective work along with protecting people. I got the impression they keep very busy."

"I'm sure they do. Frank's a former cop, so I'm guessing investigating is second nature to him. I imagine looking into threats against clients is all part of keeping them safe."

"I suppose so." She got the impression she was a special case—maybe not though.

"How's the job hunt?" Dad asked.

"Actually, I start work tomorrow for a newer ad agency. It's part time, but I'm hoping that will change soon."

"That's wonderful, Princess. I knew you'd bounce back."

"Thanks." She appreciated his faith in her, but his refusal to help her find a job still hurt. Rather than living in the lap of luxury like she had been, she was sleeping on the floor. "I need to give you my new address."

"You moved? That would explain why you weren't there when your mom stopped in to see you a couple of days ago."

"I thought I told you I lost my apartment when I was fired. It was a perk of the job."

"Oh. I don't recall that."

She gave him her new address. "What did Mom want?" They had never been close, and she couldn't recall a time when her mother had ever popped in unannounced.

"Hmm. I'm not sure."

"Well, please give her my new address, but tell her to call first to make sure I'm home."

"Will do. And you keep me apprised of your situation. I don't like the idea of you living alone while someone's making threats against you. Your mom and I talked last night and agreed you should come and stay with us until this is over."

So that's what she'd overheard. Apparently, Mom didn't want her there. Her throat thickened at the thought.

"Jenna? You still there?"

"Yes. Sorry, I was lost in thought. One of the men who works for Frank lives next to me. I'm perfectly safe here."

"Great. I feel better knowing that. I guess you're safer there, but watch your back."

"I will. Love you, Dad."

They ended their call. What was going on with her mom? One thing the past few weeks had taught her— you never really knew a person and, apparently, that applied to her mother as well.

A brushing sound against her front door made her jump. What was that? She went to the door to investigate. Footsteps sounded outside. She carefully opened the door and peeked out. A piece of paper fluttered to the ground. She grabbed the note, quickly closed and locked the door, then pulled out her phone and shot off a text to Peter.

Jenna's text kicked his pulse up a notch—another note had been left a moment ago. Peter raced to his door and yanked it open, looking both right and left. Whoever had been there was gone, but he knew for a fact this complex had security cameras.

He knocked on Jenna's door then entered when she pulled it open. "Are you okay?"

"Other than being freaked out, I'm fine."

"Where's the note?"

She held it out.

"Do you have a clear plastic bag we can put it in?"

She looked toward the boxes and her face brightened. "Yes." Within a minute she'd found the box with plastic bags inside, and he slid the note into a clear zipped bag. He read the note.

"What do you think?" Jenna asked.

"I think your letter sender knows you better than we realized. How did he know you were here?"

She shrugged. "The only person I've told is my dad, and that was a few minutes before this was slipped into the doorjamb." She reached for the bag and examined it closer. "I recognize those letters."

"Come again?"

"They were cut from a magazine spread that I was lead on. I know because I drew them by hand."

This woman constantly surprised him. "You're talented. You know calligraphy?"

She nodded. "My love of art is what drew me to becoming an ad designer. My mom and I have that in common—it might be the only thing though."

Sounded like another story, but it would have to keep. "I need to see the surveillance footage. Let's go visit the manager." He stepped forward.

She rested a hand on his forearm, stopping him. "It's after ten. We're both new here. I don't know about you, but I really don't want to get kicked out."

He scrubbed a hand along the back of his neck. "I suppose it will keep until morning." Every instinct in him said to pursue this tonight, but without a warrant or the law behind him, he was only another tenant. The manager was under no obligation to show them anything. "There's an amazing donut shop only a block away. Think I'll pick up a half dozen to sweeten up the apartment manager."

Jenna chuckled.

"What's so funny?" He couldn't think of anything to laugh about.

"You buying donuts." She emphasized the word donut.

"It's been a long day, Jenna. Help me out here."

"You're a cop, and you're buying donuts."

He dipped his chin and shook his head. "Former cop and that's so cliché." Sure, cops went to donut shops, but they also went to coffee shops and other places as well.

She laughed outright. At least she still had a sense of humor. He, on the other hand, couldn't, thanks to the latest message she'd received. He stared at the three words on the note.

I see you.

He frowned. Was this person stalking her? He clearly knew she was here and in which unit, but he'd left the other notes at her former place of employment. Why had the M.O. changed? After Peter bribed the manager with donuts, he needed to find out if any more notes were left at Ads by Design.

"You should go inside. Keep the blinds closed and stay away from the windows." He didn't want to leave her alone, but he was right on the other side of the wall. If she had a problem, he'd hear it.

"Do you think I'm safe here?"

"For now. I'm a light sleeper. If you have a problem make some noise, text, or call me."

"Hold on a second." She went to her purse then returned and handed him her spare key. "You should have this just in case."

"Good idea." He pocketed the key. "I pray it won't be necessary."

"You're a Christian?"

He nodded. His faith kept him going. In a sense, it drove him to help people. "Try and get some sleep. I'll see you in the morning." He stepped outside her apartment and waited until he heard the lock slide into place then went into his apartment, kicked off his shoes, and sprawled onto his bed. He stared at the ceiling. According to Frank, the letters began arriving the day after Jenna was let go. They'd been consistent every day until Samantha alerted Jenna about their existence. Then they'd stopped. A better friend would have warned her right away about the notes. He hoped his buddies would let him know about something like that right away.

Several friends had warned him about getting involved with Isabella, but he hadn't listened. He figured their concern lay with the fact she was a single mom. He'd been wrong. He'd sure blown it. She'd deceived him like no one else ever had, and he would pay the price for the rest of his life.

He'd felt for Isabella's situation and wanted to help but didn't see the warning signs that she was mixed up with the wrong people. He'd been blinded by her beauty and innocent act, but he'd learned a lesson, and it would never happen again.

Isabella's beauty was only skin deep. On the inside, she was as ugly as sin. His jaw clenched, and he forced himself to relax. Thinking about the biggest mistake of his life was a bad idea. He needed to chew on this new assignment—Jenna. Who was toying with her and why?

10

Wednesday morning, Jenna breezed into her new place of employment. Was it just yesterday she'd been hired? It felt much longer after the day she'd had.

Brandi sat in the one-room office behind her desk. A second desk with a computer on top had been placed directly across from Brandi's on the opposite wall. "Good morning." Jenna held up a box. "I hope you like donuts." Peter had offered her a ride to work, and they'd stopped by the donut shop on the way. She grinned. It still cracked her up that he wanted to bribe the apartment manager with donuts.

"Love them. Thanks." Brandi stood, holding a mug, and stepped over to a small coffee machine on a cart beside the restroom door. "I always brew a pot of coffee. Help yourself. There are extra mugs below."

"Thanks. I moved into my apartment yesterday and haven't yet dug out my coffeemaker." She placed the small box onto the coffee cart. Her conscience had been eating at her all night. She needed to tell Brandi about the notes but was afraid. What if Brandi let her go? No. Jenna wouldn't believe the worst. She chose a solid red mug with a large handle and filled it with a rich smelling brew. "I need to tell you something."

Brandi brought her mug to her lips. "You don't want a raise already, do you?"

Jenna grinned. "No, but if you're offering…"

Brandi laughed. "Nice try. What do you need to tell me?"

"I've hired a company that specializes in providing security for people who have had threats made against them."

Brandi's eyes widened. "I see. Are you afraid you could bring danger here?"

"Honestly, I have no idea. The notes are so vague. In fact, except for an e-mail I received at my last place of employment, there's not really a threat in any of them. It's more the way they've been presented that makes me feel threatened. Or maybe uncomfortable is a better word."

Brandi angled her head to the side. "How so?"

"Cut out letters pieced together to form words. The latest was slid under my door last night shortly after I moved in. Non-threatening but scary at the same time to think someone is watching me like that."

Brandi's eyes had grown big. "That would freak me out. What'd it say?"

"'I see you.' And the creepiest part was that the letters were cut from an ad I had created by hand.

Letters I wrote in calligraphy. I recognized my handwriting."

"That *is* creepy. How about the other ones?"

"Name-calling directed at me. Insults, that kind of thing. I assume this was all prompted by the video. I thought you should know. I hope you won't fire me now."

Brandi set her coffee onto her desk and reached for an apple fritter. She took a bite and chewed slowly. "I don't believe in letting the bad guys win." She grabbed a napkin and sat behind her desk. "Check your e-mail. I left instructions along with access codes on your desk. I need your project completed by day's end. I realize what I'm asking you to do in such a short amount of time is a lot, but your reputation precedes you. The client will be here at nine tomorrow for a presentation."

Jenna's heart skipped a beat. "I have all day to work? Not only until noon?" They'd discussed over the phone how her twenty-hour week would be scheduled, and this wasn't what they'd talked about. If she had a full day, she was certain she could pull off whatever Brandi needed.

"I've given it more thought since we last spoke. As long as I have work for you, I'd like you here all day. As it happens, I can keep you busy this week. Granted there are only two days left in the week after today. No promises about next. Is that okay?"

"It's great." Although it would make it difficult to find a second job. But if she freelanced as a graphic artist, she could do that in her off time. She got to work.

Three hours later, Brandi stood before her desk. "Mind if I see what you've come up with?"

Jenna shook her head. She had a concept and an outline, but nothing more. She stepped aside, allowing Brandi full access to her computer.

"I like where you're going. Keep it simple. Our client stressed simplicity."

"I saw that in the notes. Do you think it's too much?"

"Not yet. You ready to head out for lunch?"

She still hadn't made it to the grocery store. "I'd rather work through if that's okay. I'll have another donut."

"I believe staying fresh is key to being creative, which means a healthy lunch and fresh air. Come on. There's a great organic vegetarian place not far from here. I'll drive."

"Okay." She saved her work then stood. "That does sound better than another donut. I'm overloaded on sugar already."

Brandi locked up behind them, and they walked to her car parked nearby. "I'm curious why you hired a security firm to protect you. Based on what you told me, those letters didn't sound threatening."

"Like I said, it was mostly about how they were delivered. Plus, it was my dad's idea. I wouldn't have done that on my own." She couldn't be more grateful though. Seeing Peter again had been a huge surprise—a very nice one. She already felt safer knowing he would be right next door should she have any trouble while at home. It was funny how things had worked out. If someone had told her a month ago what her life would be like now, she would have been distraught and devastated, but these new challenges were proving to be interesting at the very least. She was stronger than she realized. Dad had been right.

"How was your first day on the job?" Peter stood in the entryway of Jenna's apartment unsure of what to do. The place was void of furniture. He knew it would be since they hadn't moved any in yesterday, but it still came as a shock to see how little she owned.

"Great. I think I'm going to like working for Brandi."

"I'm glad." He motioned in the direction of his apartment. "Would you mind if we talked at my place?"

"That's fine." She followed him out the door and locked up behind them.

A moment later, they were seated in his living room. "Because we're neighbors, and you've been unavailable to talk since you were at work all day, Frank asked me to give you an update. He checked with the local police to see if they have any open cases with a similar M.O. They don't."

She nodded. "What else?"

His gaze met hers. "You're not going to like this. Frank went to your old place of employment and spoke with," he looked at his phone, "Josh. He claims to have no surveillance that would identify the perpetrator."

Jenna cringed. "Sounds right. Samantha said the same thing. I wish Frank hadn't spoken with Josh." She sucked in her bottom lip. "I sure hope Samantha doesn't lose her job."

He shook his head. "I understand your concern for your friend, but your safety is more important than her job." Why didn't Jenna understand her friend hadn't done her any favors by not coming forward as soon as the first note was left? Anything could have happened to her during the delay.

"I suppose, but she was so nice to take me in." She shook her head as if to dismiss the topic of their discussion. "Did Frank come up with any kind of lead?"

"Not exactly. He did some digging into several of the online threats you received on social media and is looking into the more intense comments." She didn't appear to be overly surprised. "You knew about the comments?"

"Sort of. Samantha warned me they were bad and that I shouldn't look."

He raised a brow.

"What? I'm not a glutton for punishment. Plus, Brandi made me sign a contract stating I'd stay off social media."

"Do you think someone from Kratt Paper is trying to get even with you?"

She picked at a thread on her top. "Honestly, I'm surprised they haven't sued me. Then again, they wouldn't get anything since I have next to nothing. So, no. I don't think they're behind this. What would be the point? They'd have nothing to gain." She rested her head back and closed her eyes.

"You okay?" Everything in him said to comfort her, but he resisted. It was a bad idea to get too close.

She opened her eyes lazily and sat up. "Just tired. I didn't sleep well the past couple of nights, and it's catching up with me. Coffee only helps so much."

"I hear you. There's a thrift shop not far from here. I could run you over there on Saturday. Maybe you could pick up a couch. Better than sleeping on the floor."

She wrinkled her cute nose. "I don't know. What if it has bugs? I think I'll wait until I can afford something new."

"Okay." If he had anything extra, he'd send it her way, but he only had the one sofa and a chair. "What about a friend or boyfriend with extra furniture?" He looked away as the words spilled from his mouth. Talk about obvious. He'd wondered about her personal life more than once since they'd been hired. Frank had conducted an interview of her relationships before he and Sally had joined the meeting, and Peter had yet to read up on her. He needed to remedy that ASAP. She seemed so alone in the world, even with a well-known pastor for a dad.

"No boyfriend. As far as friends go, they've been quiet. I suppose that's my fault, too. I worked all the time and never made an effort. They used to invite me out for coffee and over for game nights, but I imagine I declined so often they gave up on me."

He nodded. "I understand." It had been similar for him when he was a cop. He'd grown close to some guys at the police academy, and they'd maintained their friendship until he'd turned his back on their advice. He sure missed his buddies. He'd give anything for a do-over. Then again, he never would have met Frank or Sally, or even Jenna. Not knowing them would be sad now that he knew what he'd be missing. "Good friends are hard to come by. I hope you can work things out with them."

"I don't."

He raised a brow. "That sounds like another story." She seemed to have a lot of stories to tell.

"They're old high school and college friends." She ducked her chin. "I was kind of shallow and spoiled back then and a bit full of myself. I chose friends with the same characteristics." She shrugged. "I'm not that girl anymore."

The image of her holding the tiara flashed in his mind. "Let me guess. Homecoming queen?"

She shrugged. "And prom queen."

He wasn't surprised. She was beautiful and under normal circumstances probably had charisma that surely drew others to her. "What caused you to change?"

"I'm not even sure when it happened." She looked down. "Maybe it was when that stupid video went viral. I'm not proud of myself for how I behaved, and I'm embarrassed by my outburst. Clearly, someone I worked with hates me, or that video never would have been made."

He sat up straight. "Who do you think it was?"

She raised a shoulder. "No clue. I thought we all worked well together."

"Did someone get passed over for a promotion that you received, or did you cause grief for anyone?"

She grimaced. "Maybe. I landed a few plum assignments, but we were a team."

"It's obvious someone there wasn't a team player. Think, Jenna. Who could have resented your position at Ads by Design?" They knew someone there recorded and put the video online anonymously. What if the same person had put together those letters? No, that didn't make sense. They would've known she was no longer there.

"Anyone could have harbored resentment toward me. I was handed that job without any real experience. Josh owed my dad. Lucky for all of us, I'm very good at what I do."

"Would you make a list of all the people you worked with and what their positions were?"

"Sure." She tilted her head to the side. "But I don't see what good it will do."

"Humor me." He stood and grabbed a notepad and pen from the kitchen counter then handed it to her.

"Now?"

He nodded. The sooner he ruled out her former co-workers, the sooner he could focus his attention elsewhere. Frank was following another idea.

Five minutes later, she handed him the notepad.

He looked down the page. There must be thirty people on the list. "Is this everyone?" He had his work cut out for him.

"Everyone I can remember off the top of my head." She stood. "I'm beat." She walked to his door.

He followed. "You're welcome to crash on my couch."

She glanced toward his couch and shook her head. "That's sweet, but my parents raised me to never spend the night alone at a man's house, on their couch, or otherwise."

His face heated. He'd been raised the same way but hadn't thought before making the offer. "Of course. You know where I am if you have any trouble. Want me to walk through your place before you turn in for the night?"

"It's probably not necessary, but considering everything, that's a good idea. Thanks." She followed him to her door, slipped around him, and let him into her place. She flipped the switch by the door, lighting the entryway. This apartment was too empty and gave him the creeps. He shook off the ridiculous feeling. "Stay here. I'll check the bedroom, bathroom, and closets."

He pulled open the coat closet first—empty—then moved to her bedroom. Also empty. The bathroom and shower-tub combo were equally empty. Were it not for the stack of boxes in the living room he'd think the place was vacant. "You haven't unpacked."

"I've been busy."

"Want help?" He usually zoned out in front of the TV at night. This could prove to be far more entertaining. There were few better ways to get to know someone than going through their things, and he really wanted to know Jenna. He sucked in a sharp breath. He couldn't go there with Jenna right now. She was a client and, as such, off limits.

"What's wrong?" Jenna rushed toward him. "Did you find something?"

"Everything's fine. I let my mind wander."

She shot him a questioning look. "Seems I'm not the only one with stories."

"We all have a past, Jenna." His jaw clenched. He needed to change the subject. "About the boxes."

"Right. If the offer stands to help unpack, then I accept."

He welcomed the distraction. "Absolutely." Aside from a box marked keepsakes, linens, a few kitchen items, and cleaning supplies summed up her belongings. "Do you want help with your keepsake box?"

"Sure. Would you put it in the back of the bedroom closet?"

Disappointment filled him. "You don't want to unpack it?"

She shook her head. "It's filled with silly sentimental stuff. The back of the closet will be fine."

He hoisted the box. Spasms of pain gripped his back. He gasped and set the box down.

She rushed to his side, placing a hand on his shoulder. "Are you okay? Is your back hurting you?"

He nodded, barely able to catch his breath. He needed to lie down. He sank to the floor. "I'll be okay in a little bit," he gasped out the words.

She rushed to a corner then returned holding a pillow and blanket. She spread it on the floor then helped him ease down. "What else can I do?"

"Ibuprofen."

She pulled a small bottle from her purse. "I don't have any cups unpacked."

He held out his hand, tossed the pill into his mouth, then swallowed hard, grimacing as another round of spasms attacked his back. If this episode was like any from the past, he'd be stuck in this position all night. He pulled his keys from his pocket. "I'm not going anywhere, and since I know your policy about sharing a roof, you'll need to stay at my place tonight."

"Leave you here? Alone?" Worry filled her eyes. She bit down on her bottom lip as if in a mental debate with herself.

"I'll be fine. Make yourself at home."

"Are you sure you'll be okay alone?"

Pain stabbed him. He gasped again. "Yes. Go. I have a heating pad in the closet by the door. If you could bring me that, I'll be fine."

She reached for the keys he held out. Doubt and indecision filled her eyes. "I'll get the heating pad then call Frank."

"No. Don't call him." The last thing he needed was his new boss coming here.

"I can't leave you alone."

"Yes, you can. Don't worry about the heating pad. Just take the keys and leave." He couldn't face her concern for him another moment. He was supposed to be protecting her, and here he was laid up flat—some bodyguard. "Lock up on your way out." He closed his eyes once he heard the door lock. Of all the times for his back to go out. What would he do if he still couldn't move in the morning?

11

The following morning, Jenna woke with a start. A gurgling sound filled the apartment. She sat up from her position on Peter's sofa, and the scent of coffee permeated the air. She grinned. He had his coffee set on a timer. She stood, slipped on her shoes, then went into the kitchen. A couple of mugs sat on the counter. The one shaped like a pig made her smile. "Oh, yeah. This one." She grabbed it along with a plain black mug and poured coffee into them. She didn't bother looking for creamer since she'd noticed he took it black.

A moment later, a knock sounded on the door. Her pulse picked up as she edged toward the entrance. She was being silly. It was probably Peter. "Who is it?"

"Me."

A tingle shot through her at the sound of Peter's voice. She pulled open the door and caught her breath. He looked horrible. She thrust the mug toward him. "Rough night?"

He ignored her question, took the black mug, and

shuffled past her. "Thanks. How'd you sleep?"

"The best I have in days. Thanks for the use of your couch. What can I do for you? I feel horrible that you're in pain because you were helping me."

"Just bring the mug back when you're done. Though it was intended as a gag gift, it makes me smile."

"That makes two of us. Want to trade?" She held it out.

He waved her off. "Nope. Sally is on her way over to deliver you to your office. I'm going to be a while. A hot shower is calling me."

"That's not necessary. I can take the bus or walk." She rested her hand on the doorknob and hesitated, not quite ready to leave.

"Humor me."

She sighed. "Fine and thank you for arranging a ride for me." She stood as if frozen in place. This man was something else.

He cleared his throat. "Is there something you need?"

Her face heated. "Uh, no. I hope you feel better." She started to pull the door and stopped. "Your keys are on the kitchen counter. If you need anything or a doctor recommendation, call me." She tugged the door closed.

The sun had yet to make an appearance. She shivered in the cold morning air. Thankful for the lights beside each door she slipped back into her own place. Someday, she'd like to hear the story behind the pig mug. *Lord, please heal Peter's back. He looks miserable.*

She stepped into her apartment then sipped the coffee and made a face. It desperately needed a little cream or half and half. Poor Peter, she really wanted to do something nice for him—like cook him dinner. Maybe Brandi wouldn't mind bringing her home tonight and stopping at the grocery store on the way.

With a plan for how to thank Peter, she quickly readied for work then headed out with Sally when she arrived. Twenty minutes later, she sat behind her desk and booted up her computer.

Brandi stood at the coffee station making a pot of brew. "Our client will be here at nine. I think you created a solid marketing plan."

"What about the ad itself?" She'd worked for hours on a print ad that would be placed in multiple national magazines. She had no idea how a startup company landed such a great account.

"I think he'll appreciate the simple, clean design. We'll know soon enough. Do you want to take point on this?" Brandi poured a cup of coffee then returned to her desk.

"I could, but he hired you. Aren't you afraid he'll drop you because of me?"

"If I thought that, I never would have made the offer. It's your choice."

"I think you should do the presentation. If you look like you need help, I'll jump in." Where had that come from? She'd always been assertive and never backed down from a challenge. But it wasn't about her this time. This was about Brandi—a woman who had hired her when no one else would. If Brandi succeeded, so would she.

"Okay. I know we went over all of this yesterday, but did you think of anything I should add?"

Jenna shook her head right as the door opened and a man in a business suit stepped inside. It wasn't often she saw men wearing suits, considering how casual most people dressed in the Seattle area.

Brandi stood and walked around her desk. She held out her hand. "Mr. Miles, it's great to see you again. We weren't expecting you until nine."

He shook her hand. "You as well. I'm sorry for being early, but I had to move up my timeline so I had my driver stop here first."

"Not a problem." Brandi glanced toward Jenna. "We need to set up the presentation. Would you like a cup of coffee or tea while you wait?"

"No, thanks." He parked himself in a high-backed chair near the entrance.

With a few clicks on her computer, Jenna had the presentation ready to go. She grabbed the portable screen Brandi had shown her yesterday.

Jenna set up the screen then nodded to Brandi, who appeared to be taking a moment to focus.

Jenna stayed at her desk, and Brandi stood beside the screen. She began her presentation. Jenna pressed the arrow key on her computer as Brandi went through their plan like a pro. The woman had clearly done this before.

Mr. Miles grinned and stood. "I like it. Thanks for keeping it simple. Send everything to my assistant. It was a pleasure working with you. You can count on my business in the future." He shook Brandi's hand once more then strode out.

"Yes!" Brandi pumped a fist in the air. "We did it." Her face shone with happiness.

Jenna chuckled. "You had doubts?"

"Yes. That man has a reputation for being difficult to work with. I take it your paths never crossed."

"Not that I remember." She'd worked with a large number of clients while at Ads by Design and couldn't begin to remember all of them, but if he was as difficult as Brandi stated, she'd have remembered him. She always remembered the challenging ones.

"We were the third ad company he'd come to for this particular project." Brandi put the screen away then sat at her desk.

"Wow. Okay. I didn't see that coming." Excitement filled her followed by relief. She still had the touch.

"Do you have plans for this evening?"

"Nothing firm. Why?" The thank-you meal she wanted to make for Peter crossed her mind, but she still needed to see if he was free.

"I thought we could celebrate. My best friend, Katie, and I always go out for gelato when we have something to celebrate. You're welcome to join us, assuming she's free. I need to text her and find out."

The conversation she'd had with Peter last night about friends circled around in her mind. She could use a couple of friends. "I'd love to. Can I catch a ride with you?"

"Sure."

"Do you have anything else for me to work on today?"

"Only a small project. I'll e-mail what you need to know." Brandi's keyboard clicked as she typed.

12

Carissa hung back as Hannah spoke with a friend on the local university's campus. She was beginning to think whoever had been behind the graffiti had been scared off since nothing else had happened.

Hannah turned and headed in her direction, wearing a smile.

Carissa's shoulder relaxed. That was the first time since she'd been protecting the young woman that she'd seen a genuine smile light her face. She strolled toward her client. "What's up?"

"I have a date on Saturday night."

Carissa frowned. How would that work?

"What? You seem bothered."

"Do you want me to be on this date too?"

"Of course not." Hannah chuckled. "I figured you could keep an eye out for me from afar like you've been doing today."

"That could work." The unease that the idea of a date caused wouldn't leave her. "Who's the guy?"

"It's a blind date. My friend set us up."

Carissa jerked her head to face Hannah. "Excuse me?" Hannah was a lovely person and attractive. She could certainly find her own guys to go out with.

"What?" Hannah's brow furrowed.

"Going on a blind date when you believe you're being stalked is not exactly a smart move."

Hannah waved a hand as if to brush off Carissa's concern. "I trust my friend. She wouldn't set me up with a guy like that."

Carissa shook her head. The young woman was more naïve than she had realized. "Of course, your friend wouldn't do it on purpose, but some people excel at deception."

"No way. Makayla is the most grounded and smart friend I've ever had. Besides, the person in the video was a woman, not a man." She rolled her eyes.

"The person *appeared* to be a woman." They hadn't shared Marc's theory that the graffiti artist could have been a man done up to look like a woman.

Hesitation shone in Hannah's eyes. Then they hardened. "I know you're looking out for my best interest and want to keep me safe, but you need to trust *me* this time. I know what I'm doing."

Carissa shrugged. "If you say so." The judge had sent them a check that more than covered guarding Hannah for the next month. The FBI hadn't come up with a solid lead, so Carissa would guard her, even when her client showed poor judgment.

Marc followed Makayla across campus. With any luck, Hannah's friend would fill him in about this blind date. He'd like to run a background check on the guy before the two went out.

"Excuse me," he called out to the preppy-looking brunette.

She turned and gave him a withering stare. "Yes?"

"I'm a friend of Hannah's. I was hoping you could give me the name of the guy you set her up on a blind date with. My associate and I feel like it would be best to screen him first."

"You're what? Who are you?"

He took a step back. "Hannah didn't tell you?"

"Tell me what?"

Marc hesitated. He needed to do his job, and Hannah had never said to keep what they were doing quiet. "Carissa and I are her bodyguards."

Makayla laughed. "That's crazy. You expect me to believe she has bodyguards? As if." She turned and strutted away.

He strode after her. "It's true. Ask her."

Makayla slowed and slid him a sideways look. "You're for real?"

"One hundred percent. I know you care about Hannah and wouldn't want any harm to come to her. She's determined to go on this date. Out of extreme caution, I'd like to check him out first."

Her face broke into a smile. "Cool. I know she lives with Judge Potter. Does this have something to do with her?"

"I'm not at liberty to say."

A gleam lit her brown eyes. She tore a piece of paper off a page in the notebook she carried then wrote out a name on it.

"Thanks." He looked at the name *Carson Perry.*

"He's a really nice guy and totally into Hannah. They have Lit. class together. He's kind of shy though and didn't have the courage to ask her out, so he asked me to set them up."

Marc forced a smile. He didn't like the sound of this guy already. "Any idea what his date of birth is?"

"No, but I'll find out. How will I get it to you?"

He handed her his card. "Send me a text. Thanks." The date was tomorrow night so, hopefully, she'd get it to him right away. He headed for the parking lot determined to accompany Carissa on their client's blind date. Having him there worked better anyway. Carissa could blend in better as half of a couple versus being out on her own.

He climbed into his pickup and headed for the coffee shop. Carissa would be pleased to hear he'd been successful with the friend. She'd had her doubts, but he'd been confident he could get the information from the co-ed.

Twenty minutes later, he parked and headed into Gently Brewed. A scream ripped through the air. He reached for his Glock and searched the dining area. Where were Carissa and Hannah?

The lone customer in the store stared at the gun in his hand with fear-filled eyes.

"I'm one of the good guys. Where is everyone?"

"I don't know. I was listening to my music and just notice the place had emptied when I spotted you."

"You should go. Now."

The teen girl grabbed her purse and fled the shop.

He crept toward the backroom. It was too quiet. He nudged the door only far enough to poke his head through. His stomach dropped. Carissa lay on the floor. He stepped inside with his gun drawn.

Hannah crouched behind a big box.

Marc searched the room for an intruder and found none. "I think you're safe now, Hannah."

She stood and rushed to Carissa who was stirring. "He came out of nowhere."

"Who?" His heart hammered. He should have been here. Now, more than ever, he wanted this person found and prosecuted.

"I don't know. He was hiding back here when Carissa and I came to get supplies. One minute it was the two of us; the next there was this masked man standing there. Before Carissa could respond, he bashed her in the back of the head, and she went down. When I screamed, he ran out the back door."

"Did he say anything to you or try to grab you?"

"No." Her body began to tremble. "I need to sit."

She sank to the floor beside Carissa who lay on her stomach face down.

Heart thudding, Marc checked Carissa's pulse then blew out a breath and called 9-1-1, reporting the intruder and requesting medical aid.

"I'm fine," Carissa said as she rolled over then winced. She reached a hand to the back of her head. "Don't waste an ambulance on me. If I need to, I can go see my doctor."

Marc checked her pupils—no sign of concussion. Relief washed over him. He relayed what Carissa said to the operator then turned his attention back to the ladies. "I'm going to look in the alley and see if he left any clues behind." As much as he didn't want to leave Carissa, he needed to know if the intruder lurked nearby.

He strode outside and looked both ways—no one. He went back inside. Anger surged through him. Carissa could have been killed.

The safe on the floor under a desk grabbed his attention. The door hung open. "Hannah, is the safe door supposed to be open?"

She shook her hand. "I've never seen it open. Do you think the guy was here to rob us?"

He crouched down and looked inside—empty. "That's my guess, considering he didn't seem interested in you."

"Wow." Hannah reached for Carissa's hand and helped her sit up. "Are you sure you're okay?"

"Other than a pounding headache, I think so. I'm sorry you had to deal with that on your own."

"Are you kidding?" Her pitch raised half an octave. "If it wasn't for you being here, giving me time to scream and run, who knows what would have happened. Then Marc showed up. You guys are the best."

Marc stood a little taller. "Thanks, Hannah. We're just doing our job. The police will be here any minute. You should call your manager and let her know what happened."

"Right." She pulled out her phone and made the call.

While Hannah was distracted, he checked on Carissa. "Are you sure you're okay?"

"No. I'll call my doctor in a bit. I didn't get a look at the person who hit me at all, but I know he didn't come in from the front. Are there surveillance cameras in the alley?"

"Good question." He strode outside again then looked up. Nothing. He walked to the end of the alley and noted an ATM across the street that might have a view of the alleyway. A police cruiser pulled to a stop, blocking the alleyway.

The officer got out. "Marc? You the person who called?"

"Hi, Dillon. Yes." He'd gotten to know Officer Brady while protecting Jason Wood. "There was a robbery at Gently Brewed. My associate was knocked out, and our client said the assailant wore a mask. The safe's been emptied." He pointed to the ATM across the street. "We know he didn't come in the front door. Otherwise, they would have seen him enter. There aren't security cameras in the alley, but maybe that ATM across the street caught something."

"It's possible." He spoke into his radio.

"I'll show you the scene of the crime." He directed him through the coffee shop's alley entrance.

Carissa stood in the doorway between the front of the shop and the back. There was no sign of their client. She grinned when she spotted the police officer. "Long time no see, Dillon."

"You okay? I heard you were knocked out."

"I've been better, but I expect to live." She motioned toward the front. "My client is helping a customer then I told her to close up shop until the manager arrives."

"Good. What can you tell me?" He pulled out a notebook and pen.

"Not much. I was taken by surprise. Our client can tell you more, but I don't think she'll be helpful since there wasn't much to see. If the safe hadn't been emptied, I'd have thought this was related to the case we're working."

Marc thought the same. "As soon as you've questioned Hannah, we'd like to take her home, assuming the manager is here."

"No problem."

An hour later, they left Hannah in the safety of her home along with a U.S. Marshal and the judge. Apparently, court had closed early today.

Marc turned to Carissa. "Now what?"

"Did you ever get the date of birth for her blind date?"

"Yes."

"Then run that background check on him while I go get my head checked."

Sudden concern for Carissa filled him. She was always so tough—almost invincible. He hadn't expected she'd actually go to a doctor. She must be feeling worse than he'd realized. "I can take you."

"No, thanks. I can get a taxi. I really need you to keep working. I'll touch base later."

He gently rested a hand on her shoulder. "I want to drive you. Why not take the rest of the day off? I know Frank would understand."

"It's not Frank I'm concerned about. It's Hannah. Something feels off. I won't be able to rest until I know what it is."

"Understood. Now how about we get your head checked out?"

"Okay. Thanks. I suppose you can research Hannah's date while you wait."

At ten minutes to five, the door to Jenna's office

opened and Peter walked in. A tingle zipped through her. "Hi. This is a surprise." He looked a lot better than he had when she'd seen him this morning.

"Thought you might want a ride home. I was in the area."

Jenna looked toward Brandi whose eyes twinkled mischief. "Actually, we were going out for gelato. You're more than welcome to join us."

Indecision warred on his face.

"Is there something you needed to talk with me about?"

He nodded.

"I could ride with you, and we could talk on the way. The gelato's my treat for all your help." It wasn't dinner, but she still hadn't worked out a way to get to the grocery store, so it didn't matter anyway.

He nodded. "You treated me to coffee. I think it's my turn."

"No way. I feel horrible about your back. Please let me do this. It will ease my guilty conscience."

A smile played at his lips. "Well, if it will make you feel better, then I accept."

Brandi chuckled. "Remind me not to argue with you, Jenna." She waved a hand toward the door. "Go ahead and leave. Katie and I'll meet you there soon."

"Are you sure?"

"Positive." She made a shooing motion with her hands.

Jenna quickly tidied up her desk and shut down her

computer. "See you in a little bit." She strode out the door with Peter right behind her. She slowed once they were outside. "What's going on? Did you find out who's sending the notes?"

He shook his head. With his attention drawn to all movement around them, he guided her to his white SUV.

Unease settled on Jenna. Only a short while ago, she'd been happy to see him. Now she was dreading whatever he had to say. "How's your back?"

"Much better. Sally recommended an amazing massage therapist. She gave up her appointment for me."

"That was really nice of her."

"It was a huge blessing. I feel a lot better. Sorry about last night."

"Are you kidding?" She slid into the passenger seat. "I should be the one apologizing. Your back seized up because I worked you too hard." One way or another, she'd make it up to him.

He started the engine. "Will you plug the address into my GPS?"

"Sure." She found the address on her phone then set their destination on the GPS. "All done."

He pulled out, tapping his finger on the wheel as if he was listening to an internal song, or maybe he was nervous.

She tilted her head. "What is it you needed to talk with me about?"

"Frank and I spoke with your former employer today."

Her pulse amped. "Again? But I said not to."

"I know, and I'm sorry. I reminded Frank of that, but he had some follow-up questions, and he likes face-to-face talks. Says he can read the person he's talking to better. For the record, Josh didn't know anything about the notes or any surveillance video of the notes being left."

"He's trying to protect his business. He lied. Samantha told me he said not to tell anyone, so it stands to reason he'd deny their existence."

He glanced her way then returned his focus to the road. "The thing is, Frank and I both believed him."

Weren't cops supposed to be good at reading people? "I don't understand. If Josh was telling the truth then—"

"Samantha was lying."

"But why? It doesn't make any sense."

"I don't know. There were only two sets of prints on those pages you gave Frank, and he never touched them. That leaves you and whoever left them. I have a difficult time believing letters found in an office would only have two sets of prints."

He was right. "Are you sure the other set didn't belong to Josh?"

"We are. He agreed to let Frank fingerprint him."

"Shocker. I'm surprised he did that."

"He wants this to go away." Peter glanced at the GPS.

"As in all the trouble I brought on him." She sank down in her seat.

"Presumably." He signaled and turned at a light.

"Who do you and Frank suspect?" She didn't want to consider the obvious, but what else could she think?

"We have three working theories."

She sat up and shifted to better face him as he pulled into the pizza gelato place.

"The first is that you made all this up for attention."

She gasped. "That's ridiculous. Why would I cause myself all this trouble?" They had some nerve accusing her like that. "I would *never* do something like this for attention."

"I said it's a theory, not necessarily a good one."

"Oh." Her ire eased slightly, but she was still a little miffed.

He turned off the engine and faced her. "The second is that Samantha is behind them. It stands to reason that the other set of prints have to belong to her since she gave the notes to you."

"I realize she's the obvious choice for this, but why would she do that? The person who wrote the note probably wore gloves." Though she defended her friend, doubt about Samantha lingered.

He shrugged. "I was hoping you could help me with Samantha's fingerprints."

"What's the third option?"

"Like you suggested, the person who did it wore gloves. Samantha's fingerprints will be on them because she gave them to you, and yours are obviously there too."

"But if Samantha lied about stealing them from Josh's desk…"

"It makes her look guilty."

"Did she know the location of your apartment the night the last note was delivered?"

"I didn't tell her."

He frowned. "She could have been following you."

"No way. Why would she do that?"

"Are you sure she's a friend?"

Jenna's mouth opened and closed. They hadn't been friends outside work before she'd started staying at her place. In fact, Samantha's offer to let her crash on her couch for a few days had come as a surprise. Her gaze slammed into Peter's. "I don't know. We were friendly at work. Visited in the break-room—quite a lot actually. She was easy to talk to."

"What'd you talk about?"

"Everything—family, friends, what we did over the weekend, our favorite TV shows and movies. We clicked. Sometimes we'd buy each other a cup of coffee on our way to work. We had a good working relationship. When she offered to let me stay on her couch until I got my bearings, I was astonished."

"But you stayed anyway."

Was there a hint of disapproval in his voice? "You think I shouldn't have?"

"I'm not judging. It was merely an observation."

She couldn't deal with this right now. She owed it

to Brandi to celebrate their victory today. "Right now, I want to stop having this conversation. Brandi and her friend are probably here already, and we shouldn't keep them waiting."

"Okay. We can talk later. You have to deal with this, Jenna. It's not going to go away because you don't want to talk about it."

"I know. And we will. I promise." Her stomach was so tied up in knots she probably wouldn't be able to eat, but she would fake it for Brandi's sake. Her boss deserved to celebrate, and so did she.

Peter stifled a sigh as he got out of his SUV. He didn't mean to upset Jenna. But he couldn't change the situation, and it had to be dealt with. "Are you sure it's okay that I'm here?"

"Brandi said it was, and if there's one thing I learned this week, it's that she speaks her mind. You don't have to guess what she's thinking."

He nodded. "I like people like that."

"Me too. Brandi's a good boss. I think she's going to go far in this business. She's smart, works hard, and she's courageous."

"All good qualities." He opened the door for her and spotted Brandi in line with a petite blonde.

"There they are." Jenna waved and headed for them.

He followed.

"Do you mind if I get a pizza too? My treat," Jenna said. "I have yet to go grocery shopping, and there's nothing to eat at my place."

"That's a problem we can remedy on the way back to our apartments. But I'll pay for half the pizza." He had noticed her cupboards were bare when he'd gone looking for a cup this morning before remembering she said they were still packed in a box. While in her kitchen, he'd peeked into her fridge out of curiosity— empty.

"If you insist, you can pay half. What do you like?"

"The works." He held back a smile at the small victory. She clearly liked to treat others to things.

She grinned. "I knew I liked you." She looked at Brandi and her friend, who apparently were raptly watching their interchange. "What about the two of you? Any preference?"

Brandi shook her head. "I'll eat dinner with my husband when I get home, and Katie can't have gluten."

Disappointment flashed in Jenna's eyes before she hid it with a smile.

"More for us." He rested a hand on Jenna's shoulder, noting Brandi's raised brow. He removed his hand, reminding himself that Jenna was a client. It would be very unprofessional to get involved with her personally. He was here for work. Period. Until they confirmed their suspicion about Samantha, tailing Jenna and keeping her safe was his assignment.

Jenna placed their pizza order. Then they all ordered gelato. Jenna chuckled. "My mom would flip if she saw me eating dessert before my meal."

Brandi grinned. "I think we might have the same mom."

Katie laughed. "I think it's a mom-thing in general. Don't you dare tell my kids we had dessert." She wagged a finger at Brandi. "Dinner's in the crockpot, ready to dish up as soon as I get home."

They all laughed.

Peter took a bite of his chocolate gelato. Who needed dinner when there was dessert as amazing as this? His stomach rumbled. Maybe he did.

He studied Brandi and Katie. They had an easy kind of rapport long-time friends often developed, and they showed kindness in little ways such as passing a napkin to someone before they asked for one. He liked these women. They were exactly what Jenna needed in her life.

The other two women finished off their gelato and stood after seeming to signal one another with their eyes. Brandi slipped into her jacket. "Feel free to come in late tomorrow, Jenna."

"Are you out of work for me?" Jenna's brow puckered.

"No. But you work fast, and I'm afraid I won't be able to keep you busy all day."

"Oh. Okay. How late?"

"I know we had talked about you working half-days

143

in the morning, but does it work for you to come in after lunch at one?" Brandi looped an arm through Katie's.

"I can do that."

"It was nice to meet you." Katie looked at Jenna then him. "I hope we can do this again sometime soon." They walked out arm in arm.

He glanced at Jenna who wore a crestfallen expression. "What's the matter? I thought we were celebrating."

"We are. I'm disappointed though. I'd hoped Brandi would end up needing me full time rather than only part."

He nodded. "Should I have them box up our pizza?"

"No. It won't be hot by the time we go to the grocery store and get home. Be right back. Looks like our pizza is ready." She stood and walked to the pick-up counter. A moment later she returned with their pizza.

He bowed his head and blessed the food. "Amen." He looked up and chuckled at the look of surprise on Jenna's face. "What? Your dad's a pastor. I figured I didn't need to ask permission to bless the food."

Her face relaxed. "You don't. It surprised me, that's all."

He devoured two pieces of pizza with the perfect balance of red sauce to cheese. He made a mental note to add this place to his list of favorite pizza joints. Did he dare bring up the reason he was hanging around her so much? Frank was anxious to wrap up this investigation now that they strongly suspected Samantha was behind the notes. The big question was why.

Jenna wiped her mouth with a paper napkin. "Do you want any more?"

He reached for one more slice. "This is my last one."

Her eyes twinkled. "You sure? I won't hold it against you if you want more."

"No, thanks. Take it home for dinner tomorrow."

"Good idea." She stood. "Be right back. I'll get something to put the extra in."

He took the opportunity to look around the restaurant. No one appeared to be paying her any undue attention. He finished off his last bite as Jenna returned to the table.

She packed up the pizza, and they walked outside together.

"Thanks for dinner and dessert."

"I owed you. You're a great neighbor to have next door."

He smiled and opened his vehicle's door for her. To the casual observer they'd look like a couple out on a date. He hustled around to the driver's side and hopped in. "Where to?"

"Wherever. I don't know this part of the city well."

He nodded and pulled out of the parking spot then headed toward their apartment complex. There was a

Safeway about a half-mile from their place, so it would be a good place to stop. She'd be able to manage it on her own even without a car. "What do you want to do about Samantha?"

"What do you mean?" Confusion filled her voice.

"Do you want to provide her fingerprints so we can compare them with the set on the notes? She shouldn't have touched the most recent one, so if it shows up there…"

"No. I refuse to believe she would do that. She was nice to me. Always has been. It has to be someone else. You said yourself the person could have worn gloves."

"True, but what if they didn't?" How could he help her if she refused to cooperate?

"It stands to reason that anyone who goes to the trouble of cutting out letters would have thought to wear gloves too."

Her theory was reasonable, but he felt certain Samantha was hiding something. She had at the very least lied about Josh. What else had she lied about?

13

Jenna strolled along the sidewalk in Seattle near Ads by Design. Brandi had claimed that Jenna was so efficient she'd worked her way out of a project the day before. Her Friday afternoon was clear, so Jenna decided to visit her old stomping grounds. Peter's suspicion of Samantha lay heavy on Jenna's mind since their conversation over pizza. If she hung out here long enough, she was bound to run into Samantha sooner or later.

She'd told herself she wanted scones from her favorite bakery near her old office, but maybe the seeds of doubt he had planted had more to do with her being on this block than scones. After all, she could have caught the bus that just left.

The door to the office building where she used to work opened. "There you are," she said softly.

Samantha bounded out of the building and walked briskly in the opposite direction.

"Samantha." Jenna jogged to catch up to the woman. "It's been a while. How's it going?"

Samantha did a double take. "Jenna. What are you doing here? You know Josh won't allow you in the building."

"I'm not here for Josh." She held up the bag from the bakery. "I missed my favorite scones. They also had fresh rolls that I couldn't pass up. How've you been?"

"Great."

"Do you have time for a cup of coffee?"

Samantha shook her head. "No. I need to grab lunch then get back to the office ASAP. I'm working on a big project."

"That's great. Congratulations. It sounds like business is improving. I'm really happy to hear that." Not only had Samantha not been let go, but she'd been promoted—good for her. Josh had never trusted Samantha with a big project when Jenna had worked there—at least someone had benefitted from her dismissal. "I'd love to catch up. Are you free for dinner?"

"I don't think so. If Josh found out I was socializing with you—"

"What does he have to do with our friendship?"

Samantha stepped close to the building, presumably to not block foot traffic and stopped. "Look. We aren't friends. I felt bad for your situation. That's it."

Jenna caught her breath. "But you took me in when I was at my lowest. That's what a friend does." Her gut clenched. Had she been a fool to trust her former co-worker?

Samantha rolled her eyes. "I never expected you to stay at my place for more than a couple of nights. I need to go." She took a step.

Hurt washed over Jenna as Samantha's words sunk in. "Why'd you do it?"

Samantha stopped and turned slowly. "Do what?"

"Why'd you lie about the notes?"

"I didn't."

"Yes. You did. Josh was interviewed by two former cops who say they believed he knew nothing about the notes. So why'd you lie? Were the notes even delivered to the office? Did you write them?" Her voice hitched.

"You're out of your mind. Leave me alone, Jenna, before I call the police." Samantha turned and rushed away.

Jenna stood there, unsure of what just happened. Someone bumped Jenna's shoulder, startling her from her musings. She walked to the bus stop. Samantha seemed to mean what she'd said—they weren't friends. She'd sure read that wrong. But if they weren't friends, why take her in, why pretend to like having her there, and what was the deal with the notes?

Samantha was no more her friend than the person who'd bumped her shoulder, that much was clear. But she couldn't accept that Samantha was behind those notes. That was too nuts. Her former co-worker might not be the friend she'd believed her to be, but she wasn't sadistic.

Had Josh fooled Frank and Peter? It had been more

than a week since she'd received a note. Maybe the person had tired of sending them and would leave her alone now. She sure hoped so.

Her new job was going well, and she rather liked her new normal. Living the simple life was nice. Sure, she couldn't treat people to dinner and coffee as much as she liked anymore, but there was something to be said for a small office with no competition from co-workers.

Ads by Design had been extremely competitive. Josh made no secret that if she didn't live up to expectations there was someone else who wanted her job. By the sound of it, Samantha had been that someone. That was why Jenna had been so focused and driven. She hadn't wanted to lose her job. She laughed at the irony.

Her phone vibrated, alerting her to an incoming text. She grinned when she saw it was from Peter.

How's your day off?

Odd. I'll explain later. Need to meet. Are you free?

Jenna strolled into Gently Brewed, the same place she and Peter had gone to the day she'd hired Protection Inc. She spotted him in the corner where they'd sat last time. He had two cups sitting on the table. She waved and walked over to him. "Thanks for meeting me." She sat.

"You piqued my curiosity." He handed her a cup of coffee.

"How sweet. Thanks." She sipped it and grinned. "You added cream and sugar. How'd you know?"

"I pay attention."

This guy was almost too good to be true. Her insides warmed from his care. "How is it again you aren't attached to some woman?"

He shook his head. "How about you tell me why your day was so odd?"

"Right. I ran into Samantha." Saying the woman's name brought the conversation forefront in her mind, sickening her stomach. She took a calming breath. How had she read that situation so wrong?

He raised a brow as he took a sip from his cup.

"I confronted her about Josh."

"And?"

"And she said I was out of my mind, and if I didn't leave her alone, she would call the police—" her voice caught. "Sorry. I don't mean to be emotional." She'd gone over and over that conversation on the bus ride over here, and the more she'd thought about it, the more upset she became.

He sat back in his seat. "It hurts when someone we think is genuine turns out to be anything but."

"You speak from experience?"

He nodded. A grim look settled on his face. "She's the reason I'm here."

"If you don't mind me asking, what happened?"

Pain flashed in his eyes for a moment then turned to steely resolve. "Isabella was my girlfriend."

"How'd you meet?"

"Online." He winced. "I will never do that again. My friends warned me, but I wouldn't listen. Worse yet, the Lord nudged me more than once to break it off with her, and I didn't. I knew in my heart what I needed to do, but I ignored that still, small voice."

Jenna nodded. Compassion for this kind and hurting man filled her. "I've done the same thing. It never turns out well either. So what happened that caused you to leave law enforcement and move to Seattle?"

"She used me to get some information." He sighed. "Isabella was not who I thought she was. She was on the payroll of a really bad man. She infiltrated my life, learned my habits, my schedule, and pretty much figured out how I operated. Then she used it against me." He took another drink from his coffee cup and set it down slowly.

Jenna couldn't believe someone as strong, smart, and grounded as Peter seemed to be could ever be duped. "What did she do?"

"When I had to cancel a date because of a sting, she put two and two together and alerted her boss. They were waiting for us when we showed up."

His eyebrows drew together. "We walked into an ambush. It was like a warzone, and we weren't prepared. One officer was wounded in the ensuing shootout.

Once everything settled down and we had the situation under control, I made it to the second floor to clear the rooms. It was a hot night. A large window stood open. I thought perhaps someone had jumped out and used it to escape. I went over to investigate."

Jenna leaned forward to hear his softly spoken words.

"I still don't know how Isabella got the take on me. My partner hollered at me to look out right as I was shoved through the open window."

Jenna gasped. "That's how you hurt your back."

"And ended my career as a cop. It was a long road to recovery. Internal Affairs investigated because of my relationship with Isabella. I was cleared, but I couldn't stay there. I had to move on."

"I'm sorry you went through that. It couldn't have been easy." Her heart nearly melted at the anguish on his face.

He schooled his features and focused on her. "It's in the past, but it's a lesson I will never forget."

"I imagine you're more cautious now than ever." Which begged the question, why did he believe Josh? Someone had to be lying. Peter had way more experience than she did deciphering truth from fiction. She had to believe he and Frank were right.

"I am." He finished off his coffee. "Which is why this security gig is a great fit for me. Speaking of which, have you received any more notes?"

She shook her head. "That's why I wanted to talk

with you. I think whoever is behind the notes has decided I'm not worth the effort. I'm going to end my contract with Protection Inc. I don't have the money to be chasing ghosts. My dad said he'd help with the cost, but I don't want him to have to."

He nodded, frowning. "It's a risk to discontinue our services, but I understand."

Peter's concern for Jenna quadrupled. Was money the real issue why she wanted them off her case? He studied Jenna over the top of his cup as he drank his coffee. She didn't seem overly fearful or worried.

From Peter's vantage point in the corner of the coffee shop, he could see the entire room. No one paid them any special attention, and no one drew his suspicion. Except for the occasional times Sally had been giving him a break, Peter had been following Jenna since the moment Frank had ordered him to keep an eye on her. Following city busses had been a nuisance, and he'd lost her a few times when her bus had taken bus-only routes, but he'd caught up to her at the other end. Not once had he seen anyone following her.

"Thank you for understanding," Jenna said. "I know my dad won't understand, but I imagine my mom will be relieved."

"Why's that?"

"Oh, nothing." She waved a hand and stood. "I

guess I'd better get this over with, and let Frank know his services are no longer needed. Are you headed back to your office?"

"Yep." He stood and escorted her. "Why do you suppose the notes stopped?" For the life of him, he couldn't figure it out. He expected things to escalate, not drop.

"No clue, but I'm not complaining."

He knocked on Frank's office door.

Frank waved them in. "This is a surprise, Jenna. Have a seat. Has something happened?"

"No. Which is why I've come to tell you I no longer require your services."

Frank's gaze shot to his. "I see. Are you certain? We've been looking into Kratt Paper."

"The company I besmirched? Why?"

"After we ruled out Josh, and you felt certain that Samantha wouldn't send them, we started looking into the business." He blew out a breath. "What you said about them is accurate. They are as dishonest as the rain is wet."

She chuckled. "Good luck proving it. You don't think they were sending those notes, do you? It seems so childish. Not very corporate-like, if you know what I mean."

"I do, and I agree, but we had to do due diligence. We also looked into all the other names on your list and no red flags came up. Clearly, we're missing something since the video was taken by one of them." Frank sighed. "Consider your case closed, but if you should need us at any time, please call."

She stood and offered her hand. "I can't thank you enough. I sincerely believe the worst is past. I'm ready to move forward with my future. Please send me the bill."

"Will do." Frank stood and shook her hand. "I wish you all the best." He motioned for Peter to stay put.

Jenna smiled at Peter. "Want to come over for dinner and a movie tonight? I'm celebrating a new beginning."

"I'd like that. Text me the time. See you later."

She walked out with a spring in her step he hadn't noticed before. He turned his attention back to his boss. "What's up?"

"That's my line. The two of you socialize?"

"She's my next-door neighbor, so yes."

Frank held his gaze for a moment as if sizing up his intentions.

Peter held his boss's gaze.

Frank looked down at the file on his desk then back at him. "What's your take on Jenna? I need to report to her dad."

"No one's followed her. The notes stopped a week ago." He shrugged. "She's wasting her money with us unless something else happens."

Frank nodded. "In spite of what I told Jenna, I'm concerned Kratt Paper might be behind her trouble given the backlash from her viral video, but I can't prove it." He rubbed his chin. "The thing that bothers me the most, though, is Jason Wood."

Peter tilted his head. "Someone shot at him, right?"

"Yes. And the shooter was found and arrested. I don't think Jason would stoop to sending those notes to Jenna, but I've seen too much in my life to rule him out."

"Do you have anything on him?" He leaned forward.

"Not so much as a crumb." He closed Jenna's file and set it to the side of his desk. "Moving on. I have something else for you."

Peter tried to focus on Frank, but all he could think about was Jenna. He couldn't wait until tonight.

14

Promptly at six, a knock sounded on Jenna's door. She looked around her apartment. A small round table covered with a vintage cloth sat in the dining room. After she left Protection Inc. she'd rented a pickup and visited a few thrift shops. She'd scored not only amazing stuff but muscle to help her move it. She had been totally against second-hand furniture until she'd spotted these practically new pieces.

She pulled open the door and her breath caught. Peter wore a navy sweater with gray pants and black boots. "Hi. Come in." She moved aside. "You look nice." Why hadn't she thought to put a little effort into her appearance?

He walked past her with a chuckle. "It's a step up from my normal jeans and T-shirt." He stopped moving and looked around the space. "You've been busy. None of this was here last night when I brought you home from work. How did you do all of this and still have time to make dinner?"

"When I find something I like, I know it." She shrugged. "It so happened the thrift shops had what I liked today. Plus, I found a couple of college students looking to make a few extra dollars who helped me get it up here. I hope you're hungry."

"Starved. What are we having?"

"Comfort food. Meatloaf, mashed potatoes, green beans, and fresh rolls from my favorite bakery." She watched his face for a reaction—nothing. Was he hiding that he didn't like something she had prepared? "If there's something you don't want, feel free to skip it. I won't be offended."

"Okay."

"Everything is ready. I only need to move it to the table."

"I'll help." He followed her into the small kitchen." She'd had to buy everything from the loaf pan to cook the meatloaf to the condiments. She spent more money in an afternoon than she ever had in a day. Including when she put down the deposit on this apartment. Thankfully, she had a paycheck coming soon.

Peter picked up the platter with the meatloaf and mashed potatoes and took it to the table. Jenna grabbed the basket holding the rolls and the side dish of green beans in one hand and the gravy in the other and placed them on the empty spaces on the table. There wasn't much room after the platter took up the middle.

Peter held out her chair.

"Thank you." She sat, waiting for him to join her,

then bowed her head. "Thank You, Lord, for providing this meal and the stuff to prepare it with. Thank You for Peter and his friendship. Please bless this food. Amen."

"Amen." Peter's gaze met hers. "I'm glad we're friends."

"Me too. I had forgotten what it was like to have a life. I worked non-stop at Ads by Design." She motioned to the platter in the middle. "Help yourself." She scooped up a healthy serving of green beans. "When I was a kid, my mom had a garden. We grew green beans. I've always loved them, so long as they aren't overcooked." Thankfully, she'd learned how to cook them to the perfect al dente and season them just right.

Peter took a slice of meatloaf and a spoonful of mashed potatoes then dug in.

"No green beans?"

"Ah, no, thanks." He shook his head, looking a little sheepish.

She chuckled. "Not a favorite, huh?"

"I used to gag those down at the dinner table as a kid before I could have dessert. I'm sure yours are good, but I can't." He cringed.

She laughed. "It's okay." She forked one into her mouth. "Mmm."

He laughed and shook his head. "Don't try and tempt me. It won't work."

"More for me." She took another bite and made a silly face.

"Better watch it, I'm not above a food fight." He held up a fork loaded with meatloaf.

She sobered. "Okay, fine. I'll behave, Mr. Killjoy."

"Not fair. I know how to have fun. In fact, I thought we could watch a comedy tonight"

He grinned. He took several bites of his meatloaf. "This is actually really good."

She chuckled. "You doubted?"

"Kind of. I figured a career woman like you wouldn't have time to learn to cook. Plus, when we moved in your boxes, none of them were marked kitchen or pots and pans."

"That's because my old apartment came completely furnished. There was no need to waste money. I did have a set of cups I picked up at one of those home shows, but that's pretty much all I had already."

He reached for his cup filled with water.

"And it so happens my mom insisted I learn to cook when I was a kid. I've been working in the kitchen for as long as I can remember. Mom started with baking lessons, which I loved. Then as I grew older, maybe seven or eight, I started helping with the meals."

"Impressive."

She shrugged. "It's not a big deal. Lots of kids cook with their parents."

"I suppose." He finished the food on his plate then sat back in his chair. "Thank you for dinner. Looks like you're done too."

She looked down at her empty plate. Somehow,

she'd managed to demolish her meal without realizing it. Peter was quite a distraction. Hmm… "Movie time."

"What about the dishes?" He stood, holding his plate.

"Put them in the sink. I'll take care of them later."

She hated washing dishes and didn't want anything to spoil tonight. Aside from her encounter with Samantha, today had been a great day, and she planned to end it that way. For the first time in a month, her life finally felt right. She passed Peter on her way to the sink as he was leaving the kitchen.

"Uh, Jenna? Where's your TV?"

She gasped, set her dishes in the sink, and slunk out to the living room where no television sat. "I forgot to buy one."

He tossed his head back and laughed.

"It's not funny. I tried to be Pinterest perfect, and I left off the TV."

He sobered and walked toward her. "Hey. I'm sorry. I didn't mean to hurt your feelings. I know you worked hard to pull off tonight. I honestly don't know how you managed to do all you did in only four hours. Something was bound to be forgotten. Let's go to my place. I'll make popcorn."

She couldn't move. Her feet felt cemented to the floor. "I really wanted to do this for you to thank you for being there for me."

He stuffed his hands in his pockets. "It was my job."

Her face heated. Of course, he hadn't spent all that time with her simply because he wanted to. He'd done it because she'd hired the company he worked for to protect her and look into the letters she'd received. She'd been such a silly fool to think he'd helped her out of the kindness of his heart. But he wasn't on the clock now, so why was he here?

Concern for Jenna consumed Peter as he sat beside her on his sofa. She hadn't said much since he opened his big mouth, saying that spending time with her was his job. The hurt that immediately covered her face would have clued in even the most clueless that her feelings were hurt. He glanced her way again. She sat rigid, staring at the TV.

He grabbed the remote and pressed pause. "Jenna," he said softly.

"Hmm?" She still faced the screen.

"Please look at me."

She tilted her head his way.

"I'm sorry."

"For what? You haven't done anything wrong."

"Yes, I did. I wasn't completely honest with you earlier. Yes, my job was to make sure you stayed safe, and yes, whenever I was with you, it was technically part of my job, but I didn't have to be with you. I could have protected you from afar."

She peeked at him. "Then why didn't you?"

Good question. He couldn't tell her he felt sorry for her and wanted to help her. That would only make her angry. "I wanted to. I enjoy your company, and it was easier to be a part of your life than watch from the outside." He'd learned a lot about her in the time he'd followed her. First and foremost, she had no life. As in she had nothing—no friends, unless you counted her new boss, no outside activities. She didn't even go to church on Sunday. Sure, she had family, but you wouldn't know it from following her.

Her shoulders relaxed. "Oh. I like your company too."

He grinned. "Good. Now that that's settled. How about we actually watch the movie rather than pretend."

She nodded. "I'd like that, but it's getting late. I should go." She yawned and stood.

"Why? Do you work tomorrow?"

"No. It's Saturday."

"Then what's your rush? Let's finish the movie." He grasped her hand and gently tugged. "Come on. Sit with me. I like the ending. It's almost over."

"I guess a little longer will be okay. I told my parents I'd go to their house tomorrow morning for brunch."

"Special occasion?"

"Nope. I need them to see that I'm okay." She sighed. "I might as well tell you. Remember the day I hired Protection Inc.?"

He nodded. He'd never forget.

"Well, the night before that, I'd gone home to stay with my parents because I was scared. When I got there, I could hear them arguing from outside the front door. They were arguing about me. Mom basically accused my dad of spoiling me. I've never heard them argue like that. Much less argue about me. I haven't been home since or spoken with my mom."

His heart hurt for her. He wanted to make everything better for her, but couldn't. Give him a crime to solve or protection duty and he'd rock, but not so much with family stuff. "So they don't know you overheard their argument?"

"No. I'm not sure I want them to know, but I need my mom to see that I'm making it on my own."

"I get that. I hope it goes well." Making it on his own had been a huge motivation in his life too—especially after Isabella. Aside from the hour-long commute, independence was the reason why he chose to live in an apartment rather than his home in Warm Beach—though legally his house, it still felt like his aunt's place. Aunt Charlotte was like a second mother to him, and one day, he might move north, but right now he needed to make it on his own.

"Me too. I've always thought my mom and I got along okay. We aren't close, but I never imagined she thought the way she did. It hurts."

"I can see that." He pulled her against his side into a hug. "You've got this. You're strong, and from what

I've witnessed, you can hold your own with anyone."

"Thanks. I appreciate that. Now are we going to finish this movie or not?"

Right, the movie.

15

Saturday night, Carissa sat beside Marc at a small table in a hole-in-the-wall family-run restaurant with a barely touched large bowl of spaghetti and meatballs between them. When she'd placed the order, she couldn't help but think of the movie with the dogs eating a bowl of spaghetti between them—a childhood favorite.

Hannah visited with her date two tables away—far enough Carson wouldn't realize they were guarding her yet close enough to react in case of trouble. Carissa had called ahead to arrange the seating.

Her head still hurt, but the doctor had cleared her to work on the condition she took it easy. Well, that would all depend on Hannah's date. Hopefully, the guy wouldn't cause any trouble.

Marc leaned close. "I know this Carson guy checked out, but I still don't like him."

Carissa rested a hand on his forearm. "What is it that bothers you?" She kept her attention focused on everyone around them, watching for trouble like always.

"The I'm-too-shy-to-ask-her-out thing. I don't buy it. Look at him. Does he look shy to you?"

She studied Carson for a moment. "Now that you mention it, no. Though he seems a little nervous. Do you think he has an ulterior motive?" She looked toward Hannah who glanced toward her with a look of panic in her eyes. "Something's wrong." She stood. "Cover me." She grabbed her water goblet and strode toward Hannah's table then *accidently* dumped the contents of her goblet on Carson.

Carson leapt from his seat, allowing the excess water to pour off him. "Watch what you're doing."

Hannah stood. "I'll get some napkins."

Carissa fussed over Carson while Marc diverted Hannah to the hall leading to the emergency exit. She'd give about anything to hear that conversation. "I'm so sorry. I don't know what happened. Your girlfriend should be back any minute with some napkins."

"She's not my girlfriend." He scowled.

"No? You look like such a great couple."

"Then the joke's on you. I have a girlfriend."

"Then I take back my apology. What kind of man cheats on his girl? Men like you disgust me." Maybe she was laying it on thick, but she wanted to rattle him.

His face reddened. "Chill. It's not what it looks like. I'm short on rent money. Someone paid me to get her to come out with me tonight. Good money, too."

Carissa's pulse quickened. "Is that so? Then I guess

the joke is really on you." She pulled out her business card. "I can have the authorities here with one quick phone call."

"I didn't do anything wrong." He crossed his arms. "You're bluffing."

"You care to find out?" She pulled her phone from her pocket and pressed the number for the U.S. Marshal watching the judge tonight. "I have a situation. Turns out Hannah's blind date was paid to ask her out."

"You're kidding?" Marshal Jennings said. "Makes me wonder if the target was your girl all along or if someone is using her as a way to get to the judge."

"I don't know, but I thought you should be aware of the situation."

"Hannah left her itinerary. I'll have a marshal there soon. Detain him."

The smug look on Carson's face faded.

"You heard that, huh?"

He nodded and sank into his seat. "Am I in trouble?"

"That remains to be seen." She dropped onto the seat beside him. "What were you thinking? Did it not occur to you that you could be endangering Hannah by agreeing to this?"

He shrugged.

"How much were you paid?"

"Five hundred dollars." He hesitated. "You'll probably find this out anyway, so I might as well come clean." He pulled a pill from his pocket. "I was supposed to make sure she took this at the end of our date. The guy said he was playing a practical joke. I didn't think anyone would get hurt."

Carissa clenched her jaw biting back a curse. "You didn't think is right."

"Look, it's not like I went through with it. That ought to count for something."

"Not much. Who's this person who paid you?"

He pressed his lips together.

Carissa shot off a text to Marc, updating him on the situation. Then read his reply.

Taking her home. Be back soon.

Carissa sighed and focused on Carson. This night had not gone how she'd hoped it would. "A U.S. Marshal is going to walk in that door any minute, and you will be expected to cooperate."

He nodded then shot from his seat and raced for the door.

"Are you kidding me?" She started to go after him but stopped when the marshal—all six-plus-feet of muscled body, blocked the exit.

Carson's shoulders slumped. He turned and walked back to the table.

"Sit," the marshal said. He looked at Carissa. "Thanks for calling. I've got it from here."

She stifled a sigh. "Will you read me in later? My client's life could depend on it."

His steely look gave nothing away. Clearly, the man wasn't in the mood to play nice. That was fine. She'd learn what she needed from the judge. The woman had a way of knowing everything about everyone around her.

She had ridden here with Marc, so she was stuck until he returned. Now what? Her meal sat untouched. No way could she eat all of that. She'd have most of it boxed up and take her time with the rest. Maybe by then she'd know something, or Marc would return for her.

An hour later, Marc walked in and joined her. The marshal and Carson had left thirty minutes prior. Carson had looked green. She hoped he'd been scared enough to never do anything like that again.

"Sorry it took so long. The judge demanded we tell her everything."

"What did Hannah have to say?"

"She said the date had started off okay. Then something Carson said set off an alarm in her mind, and that's when you jumped in."

"What did he say?" She'd been stewing over what had tipped Hannah off to trouble for the past hour and had yet to figure it out.

"He said his girlfriend had the same earrings she was wearing."

Carissa shook her head. "Go figure. The moron gave himself away."

"I take it you were unimpressed with him." Marc smirked.

"That's putting it mildly. Your instincts were spot-on about that guy."

"Thanks. I wish I'd been wrong, though. Hannah's pretty upset."

"And she doesn't even know about the pill. The biggest question of all, though, is who paid him to do it? And what did he have planned for Hannah after she took the pill?"

"Do you believe Carson was telling the truth about that? What if he made it all up to make himself look not so guilty?"

"Then he's a better liar than I thought. I imagine we'll know soon if he was telling the truth or not. The marshal sent to talk to Carson took him into custody about thirty minutes before you arrived. You want to get out of here? I had most of our meal boxed, and they're keeping it in the kitchen."

"You ate?"

"Yep. Be right back." She got up and spoke to their waitress and returned a couple of minutes later with their food. "Let's go to my place. Maybe watch a movie?"

He grinned. "I like how you think."

Marc glanced toward Carissa as she sat beside him in the cab of his pickup on the way to her place. "How're you doing?"

"Fine."

"Are you sleeping okay?" The dark circles she'd

tried to hide with makeup already answered his question, but he hoped she'd confide in him.

She sighed. "Sleep is elusive. I can't help but feel like we're missing something."

"If we are, so are the marshals." Then it was the case keeping her awake, not nightmares—good. He'd lost some sleep over Hannah's situation as well. "Have you ruled out the screenwriter?"

"Yes. Although Willy did seem suspicious to begin with, I don't think he's our perpetrator. Whoever's toying with Hannah wants to hurt her. It feels personal. I think it's someone she knows."

"As in a friend?" Marc hadn't considered that angle.

"Probably not a close friend. More than likely an acquaintance. Someone Hannah knows enough to have offended but not so well she'd ever think of this person if we asked."

"Completely not helpful." He gripped the steering wheel tight. What if it was someone from the coffee shop? Someone who might be jealous of Hannah. What would they be jealous of? Then again, Carissa could be onto something. Maybe Hannah had offended a co-worker or classmate. People were offended so easily. It wouldn't be hard to do. "I think it's time for operation dig."

Carissa chuckled. "What does that stand for?"

"As in dig into Hannah's life. Find out things her own mother wouldn't know."

Carissa groaned. "You know I hate research."

"Leave it to me. I'll get Sally to help. She excels at burrowing into people lives."

"Perfect. In the meantime, you better slow down, or you're going to miss my street."

He hit the brakes and signaled. "Sorry. I wasn't paying attention."

"I noticed, but I'll forgive you." She reached over and took his hand, threading her fingers through his and resting it between them. "I'm looking forward to snuggling on the couch and watching a movie together."

"Me too." He missed this. Lately, it had felt like they were nothing more than best friends and co-workers. They needed some downtime—soon. One way or another they'd have to find time for them or risk there not being a *them* anymore.

16

The following morning Jenna sat at the dining room table in her parents' home. Since when did her visits justify pulling out the fancy dishes? They normally ate at the kitchen island.

Mom shot her a nervous smile as she handed her a platter piled high with pancakes. There was no way the three of them would be able to consume all of those. Plus, there was a bowl filled with scrambled eggs and a plate of bacon.

Jenna took the platter and placed two pancakes onto her plate. "These look and smell delicious, Mom. What's the special occasion?"

"There isn't one. It's been awhile since we sat in here, and I thought it'd be a nice change."

"It is. Great idea." Something was up with Mom, and Jenna aimed to discover what. "How did the board meeting go, Dad? I'm sorry I forgot to ask sooner."

"We missed you at Sunday service last week." Dad sipped his coffee.

She glanced at her mom. "Okay, what's going on? The two of you aren't acting right. Mom only cooks like this when she's uptight, and Dad you completely avoided my question."

Dad sighed and set his cup on the table. "If you'd been at the service last week, you'd have already heard."

"Heard what?"

"I resigned."

It felt as if all the air had been sucked from the room, and time seemed to stand still for a moment. She blinked rapidly. "For real? Why?"

"The board members felt it was for the best. To be honest, I sensed this coming on for some time. They've been pushing for changes at the church that I've resisted. The situation with you gave them fuel to push harder."

Her heart hammered as the reality of his words hit her. "You lost your job because of me? That's not fair. I'm an adult, and I'm responsible for my own actions. Not you."

"Nonetheless, it's done, and I'm not sorry. It was time. I was restless, and you know how I have a hard time quitting something. What happened was for the best. Don't blame yourself. It's not your fault. I believe this is ultimately a good thing."

She looked to her mother whose lips were pressed tightly together. The day she'd overheard their argument was the same day as the board meeting. Her mom probably had been speaking out of anger. Jenna's eyes watered as everything fell into place. "I'll talk to them. I'll even go before the church and apologize. Dad, you love being a pastor. You can't let them do this to you."

"You're not hearing me. I'm not sorry about how things turned out. I'm ready for something new," he said slowly and firmly.

She blinked. He was serious. How had she not noticed he was discontent? Then again, she hadn't been around much and had been very focused on her own life. "What will you do? It's not like they paid you an excessive amount of money."

"The house is paid for. We don't need much. Your mom's been selling her paintings at art festivals for the past few summers and has quite a nest egg."

Her gaze whipped toward Mom, and she grinned. "Way to go, Mom. I saw that you were painting again but had no idea."

Mom's lips parted. "How did you know? I've kept it quiet."

"I noticed when I spent the night in my old playhouse one night not too long ago. But why keep that you're painting again quiet? You have talent."

"Thank you." Mom's brow furrowed. "Now back to you spending the night in my studio. Why would you do that?"

Jenna looked down. She hadn't planned to tell them about that night, but she needed to come clean. "I had hoped to stay here after I received those letters, but then I heard you arguing about me when I was about to knock on the front door. I thought it best to not interrupt so I spent the night there."

Her mom gasped. "Oh, Jenna. I was angry and hurt that night. Please don't—"

"It's okay, Mom. You're talking to the queen of ranting. I understand the situation now and why you were upset." Forgiving Mom was easy but forgiving the church, that was a different matter entirely. She didn't care if her dad thought this was a good thing or not—it wasn't fair.

"Are you sure you're okay?" Mom reached over and grasped Jenna's hand.

"You and I are fine. But to be honest, I'm furious at what our church did to Dad. It's the only church I've ever gone to. I can't believe the board did that."

"Me either, but you know what? After Dad and I calmed down, we realized this is a good thing." Where worry had crowded her mother's eyes before, happiness filled them now. "We're both tired and ready for a change." She chuckled. "I think the Lord has been nudging us for a while, but we were too stubborn to listen."

"Are you suggesting that since you didn't listen, God allowed the board to force Dad to leave?"

"Now hold on. Dad was not forced to do anything. Had he put his foot down, he'd still be there. He finally listened and obeyed. Sure, I didn't like how it happened, but I'm excited about what's to come. We're going to get a small camper and travel together to art festivals with my work. We'll go all over the country. It'll be fun." She looked lovingly at Dad.

The tension in Jenna's shoulders eased. "That does sound like fun. Kind of romantic too."

Her mom giggled.

Jenna chuckled with relief. In spite of everything, she was happy for her parents. "You two kids are going to be just fine."

Her mom's eyes widened as she crumpled a napkin and tossed it at Jenna. "We are not children, missy."

Jenna looked pointedly at the napkin her mom had tossed. "Oh, really?"

They all burst out in laughter.

Mom sobered. "I didn't spend the past hour in the kitchen so we could eat a cold meal."

Her dad looked at their untouched food. "Uh, hon. I think it might be too late."

Mom stood. "Well grab your plates. We can re-heat them in the microwave."

And just like that, they were one small, happy family again. Though anger still simmered in Jenna, she would not ruin this time with her parents. It had been forever since she'd seen them so relaxed and carefree.

Peter heard the door to Jenna's apartment close. Ever since arriving home from church, he'd been watching for her to return from her visit with her parents. Having sensed her apprehension and tension about her visit last night, he'd prayed their time together went well.

He waited five minutes then grabbed the box of donuts he'd picked up earlier and went next door. Before he could knock, the door opened.

Jenna screamed and slapped her hand over her mouth. She slowly eased her hands to her sides. "Peter King, what are you doing standing there?" Her gaze lowered. "Are those donuts?"

"Yes, and I was getting ready to knock. I'm sorry to startle you."

"It's fine. I was headed out though."

"Already? I thought you just got home."

She raised a brow. "Are you still keeping an eye on me?"

"No." His face heated. "I only wanted to know how it went with your parents." He stepped back. "I won't keep you. We can catch up later."

She shook her head and opened the door wider. "I'm not in a rush. Besides, you brought donuts, which I can eat any time of day."

He grinned and handed her the box then walked inside and waited for her before sitting on the sofa. "How was brunch with your parents?"

She pulled a glazed donut from the box, took a bite, and chewed slowly. She finally stopped chewing and set down the treat. "It was enlightening." She sat on the other corner of the sofa.

"How so?"

"My dad resigned. He and my mom will be traveling the country selling her paintings at art shows during the festival season."

"What will he do in between?"

"I didn't ask. It was all such a shock. I feel like it's my fault." Her eyes welled up, and tears spilled down her face. With a tear-choked voice she told him about her conversation with her parents and how she was the reason behind his resignation.

Concern consumed him, and he moved to her side, pulling her into his embrace. He held her, letting her cry until she was done. He lowered his arms and pulled several tissues from the box on the coffee table.

She wiped her eyes and blew her nose. "Thanks. I'm sorry. I didn't mean for that to happen."

"There's no need to apologize. Is there anything I can do to help?"

"Not really. Thanks for not trying to fix me."

He chuckled. "I'm no good at fixing people." The way he saw it he was as imperfect as the next person and had no business giving her advice.

She knew what she said at her old job was wrong. It really was too bad someone at her office had been so vindictive. They hurt a lot of people. He'd sure like to know who had done that. The cyber-crimes division where he used to work could probably track the person who uploaded the video. Why hadn't he thought of that sooner?

Jenna met his gaze. "What? You have an I-just-thought-of–something look on your face."

"Did anyone try to track the ISP of the person who uploaded the video of your rant?"

"I thought Frank mentioned something about trying, but I can't remember for sure. He never indicated he'd been successful if he did. I know *I* didn't try." The confusion on her face cleared. "Do you think we can find out who did it?"

"Unless they were on a public computer, it's a good possibility."

"How?"

"I have a friend who might be able to help us."

"A cop?"

He shook his head. "No. But the department consulted with him once on an especially difficult case."

Her face lit. "If we find out who did this then…" She frowned, "Nothing. It won't make any difference. It doesn't change what happened or the damage it caused. My dad still resigned. I still lost my job, and my reputation is still tarnished."

He leaned forward, resting his elbows on his knees. "All true, but wouldn't you like to know who did this to you?"

Silence met his question. How could she not want to know? "Maybe that person was behind the notes."

"But they stopped. Do we really want to stir up more trouble by looking for him? Say we find him and confront him? What then?"

"Then we determine if he means you any more harm."

"I don't know." She shook her head and stood. "No. I want this to go away. If you start digging, it could all start up again. I need to touch up my face then head out."

He stood. "I didn't mean to upset you, Jenna, but I have to disagree. Until we know who was behind all of this, you will always wonder. How will you know who to trust?"

"I guess I'll have to rely on my instinct. Please let this go." She pleaded with him.

Doing so was a bad idea. "If you change your mind, let me know."

"I won't."

He nodded and left. She might not want to know who betrayed her, but he did. He went back to his apartment and made a call.

17

Monday morning, Jenna stood at the coffee cart at work and poured a cup of rich-scented brew. Brandi had called her in early because she'd landed an account and a project for Jenna.

Brandi leaned against her desk, sipping from a mug of her own. "How was your weekend?"

Jenna looked at her over the top of her mug and decided to trust her. She could use a girl's perspective. Peter was a sweetheart, but he thought like a man not a woman. "It was filled with ups and downs. Do you mind if I get personal?"

Brandi raised a brow. "Not at all. Will it be quick, or should we plan to talk at lunch?"

Jenna nodded. "Lunch might be better." She hadn't planned to share her personal life with Brandi, but she was so easy to talk to, and most important, she was real. You never had to guess with her. Jenna went to her desk and got to work on her latest project.

Three hours later, Brandi stood and stretched. "The morning flew. You ready to get lunch?"

Jenna noted her boss's lunch bag on the shelf behind her desk. "Did you pack one today?"

"I did, but we can go out."

"I brought mine too. We could talk here if that's okay. I'd rather not be overheard by anyone."

"Sure." Brandi pushed some papers aside.

Jenna made space on her desk for her meal then pulled out a peanut butter and honey sandwich.

"What was it you wanted to talk about?" Brandi opened her lunch bag and dug out a salad and fork.

"I learned this weekend that the church board where my dad is, or rather was, the minister, asked him to resign. I'm so angry. I don't know what to do."

"Why'd they ask him to resign?"

"Because of me. It's so unfair to my parents. They've given their lives to serving there. I mess up, and they pay the price."

Brandi blew out a breath. "That's rough. I agree it's not fair."

"Thanks. I don't like feeling this way, but I'm not sure how to get past the anger and forgive them. I know that being human means we mess up. I'm the perfect example, but my dad is innocent. To top it all, my dad is okay with it. He said he was ready for a change, and it gave him the kick in the pants he needed to move on to something new—my words, not his."

"It sounds like it all worked out for the best for him, and he's happy."

"That's not the point." Jenna blew out a breath. She

needed to calm down. "The point is, he shouldn't have been let go because of me."

Brandi nodded. "I don't want to sound trite, but have you prayed about this? I think sometimes only the Lord can heal a wound like yours. This might be one of those times." She shrugged. "Here's something to consider. I believe that sometimes He allows us to be in a rough situation to help us realize we've deviated from walking the path He has for us."

Hmm. She hadn't thought about the situation that way. "Do you think praying would help?"

"It sure wouldn't hurt. How are your parents doing?"

"Better than I would expect."

Brandi smiled. "That's wonderful."

"I agree." She'd been thinking the same thing, but the reason behind it still upset her. "The change is definitely good, but it's still hard to accept." People needed to mind their own business and stop judging others.

"How are things going with Peter?"

"What do you mean?"

"The chemistry between the two of you is impossible to miss."

Jenna grinned. "He's great, but I don't think he cares for me like that. I feel like we're firmly in the friend zone."

"Really? That wasn't the impression I had the other day. What about you? How do you feel?"

"I'm interested, but…"

"But what? This is the twenty-first century. A woman can ask a man out without raising eyebrows."

"I kind of already did." Jenna laughed. "But my life is too messy to drag him into it."

"Life *is* messy. There's nothing you can do about it. Why not let him decide if it's too messy or not?"

"Because I don't want to." If she opened her heart and he rejected her, it would be too much after everything else that had happened.

"Okay. I didn't mean to push. Want to hear how I met Ian?"

"Absolutely." She'd welcome the change in subject.

"It was a rainy fall Saturday morning near Green Lake. I had just purchased my favorite coffee drink and stepped outside. There was a huge puddle in the road."

Jenna gasped. "Oh no." She could see it now.

"Oh yes. He drove through the puddle, sending a wall of water over the top of me. I was soaked, and my coffee was ruined."

"Not the coffee!"

Brandi grinned. "Devastating, I know."

"What happened next? How'd you meet?"

"He got out, apologized, and offered to buy me another coffee. We really clicked, except for one thing."

"What?" Jenna asked.

"I was on a six-month sabbatical from dating that didn't end until Christmas."

"But you dated him anyway, right?"

Brandi shook her head. "No. I made a promise to

God, and I always keep my promises. I needed to discover me again. I had a habit of bouncing from one guy to the next and in the process lost myself and had drifted away from the Lord. I had devoted those six months to growing my relationship with Him without the distraction of dating."

Jenna almost blurted "that's insane" but caught herself in time. Brandi didn't judge her, and she would return the favor. "So how did you end up together?"

Brandi glanced at the clock. "That's a story for another day. Lunch is over."

"Slave driver," Jenna teased.

"Ha ha. This was fun."

"Are you sure about this?" Peter rubbed the back of his neck as he spoke into his phone. The clock on his kitchen wall ticked off the seconds. He'd hoped Doug Slone, the consultant for the cybercrimes department, would be able to track the ISP for the video of Jenna, but he hadn't expected this.

"Positive. The video was uploaded from a phone registered to Ads by Design."

"Any idea who specifically uses the phone?"

"That information isn't available." Doug started to explain how the person did the deed, but Peter had no idea what he was saying—computers were a foreign language to him.

"Hey, thanks for everything. I owe you."

"Sure thing. Good luck."

The call ended.

Peter needed more than luck. He needed a miracle. A knock at his apartment door drew his attention. He stood and answered it. "Jenna, this is a surprise."

She held a pizza box. "I hope I'm not interrupting something." She looked past him into his apartment.

"Not at all. What's up?"

Her forehead furrowed. "Uh. I just wanted to say hi. See how things are going."

He nodded toward the box. "Are you going to eat that whole pizza by yourself?"

The strain on her face eased. "Not if you want to share."

"Sounds good to me. I haven't had dinner yet."

A smile lit her face.

He opened the door wide and stepped aside. It was interesting that she showed up at his door right after his conversation with Doug. "Come in."

"Thanks." She walked over to his table and set the box down. "I got the works." She opened the box and sat.

"My favorite." He grabbed two plates and poured two cups of ice water. "How was your day?"

"Fun. Brandi gave me a new project. How about your day?"

"Interesting. I spent most of it doing research." He reached for his cup. "I'm going away for a couple of days." He wasn't crazy about it either since it would mean he wouldn't be here for Jenna if she needed him, but she was no longer his client, and Frank assigned him to protection duty for another musician. What was it with musicians needing security?

"Will you be home at all?"

"I'll be with my client until he leaves Seattle."

Disappointment clouded her eyes. "Lucky client."

"Wasn't all that long ago you were my client." He grinned, thrilled that she would miss him and wasn't afraid to let him know. He'd sure miss her. He'd pushed aside his attraction to her because she was his client, but there was nothing keeping him from asking her out now except lack of time. Would she resent the crazy hours he worked? His gaze flicked to hers, assessing. He shook his head. Now wasn't the right time.

"Where'd you go?" Jenna asked with a teasing glint in her eyes.

"Sorry. I was lost in thought. How does your mom like having your dad around all the time now?"

She shrugged. "I don't know. I didn't think to ask. I know she spends a lot of time in her art studio, painting. Funny, when my dad was a pastor he would be called away at all hours. We were used to him not being home rather than being home. I imagine it's quite a change for both of them."

"Did it bother you that he wasn't around?"

"Only when he missed important things, like a birthday party or a school function. Honestly, I've never known a different life. So I guess having him around all the time would feel really weird." She took a bite of her pizza. "Actually, when my mom was talking about their plans, she seemed pretty excited. I think my dad's going to have more of an adjustment than she will. She still does her own thing."

He nodded. It sounded like Jenna wouldn't mind his crazy schedule if she was used to her dad having one. Did he dare risk asking her out?

"Do you go to church anywhere?"

He blinked. "I'm still looking for a good fit."

"Oh. I was hoping for a recommendation."

"You're not going to go back to your church?"

Her jaw set, and an angry glint flashed in her eyes. "No way. Not after what they did."

"I see. You're welcome to try out churches with me. Thought I'd check out the community church a few blocks from here this week."

"I'd like that. Thanks."

He ducked his head and took another bite. He understood the anger he read in her eyes. "Do you mind a little unsolicited advice?"

"I guess not." She looked ill at ease.

He'd better tread carefully. "I told you the story about how Isabella pushed me out that window."

She nodded.

"The thing is, I trusted her. Cared about her. She betrayed me and used me to her own gain. It really hurt and made me angry."

"I can relate."

"I know. It's been difficult to get past the anger and doubt."

"Doubt?"

He nodded. "Yes. As a cop I had to trust my instincts. My life and my partner's life depended on it. Yet Isabella fooled me. She didn't fool my friends though. They warned me, and I didn't listen. So, yes, I've had a hard time trusting my gut since. I doubt my instincts now. I should've listened to my friend's warnings."

"Are you doing better?"

"I'm cautious, but yes, I think so. As far as the anger goes, it still flares up from time to time if I dwell on it. But here's the thing about holding onto anger." He waited for her to meet his gaze. "It festers and turns ugly. I don't want that in my life. I want the fruit of the Spirit: love, joy, peace, patience, kindness, goodness, gentleness, and self-control. It's difficult to have any of those qualities when I'm letting anger fester."

She slowly chewed the pizza she'd been working on. "I've been so angry lately. I definitely haven't felt very joyful or peaceful."

"Then let go of the anger."

"Easier said than done." She waved her hand toward the pizza. "Would you like more?"

"No, thanks."

She closed the box and stood. "I won't hijack your evening. Be safe this week."

He stood and walked with her to the door. "I'll do my best. And, Jenna?"

She looked up at him.

"Watch your back."

"You still think I'm in danger?"

"I think watching your back is always a good idea, but especially when you've made someone angry."

"The whole festering thing?"

He chuckled. "Yeah, I suppose so." He hadn't thought about that but it fit.

"Okay. See you."

He stood in his doorway and waited there until she went into her apartment and closed the door. Then he shut his and returned to his notes. What did he do now?

18

Marc pulled up a chair and sat beside Sally at her desk. "What do you know?"

"I looked into the judge like you requested."

"And?"

"I can't find any record of her giving birth, but her twin sister did and look at this," she handed him a piece of paper. "It's the same year Hannah was born."

He skimmed down the birth record. It didn't tell him anything helpful.

"The baby girl was adopted in a closed adoption. We can't know for certain, but it looks possible that Judge Potter is Hannah's aunt. That would explain why she'd allow a random college student to rent a room from her."

"It would, but we can't prove it, and even if we could, what difference would it make?" He asked.

"Maybe none, but what if someone found out Hannah is her niece and is using her to get to the judge? Or maybe they want to abduct her and hold her for ransom, knowing the judge could and would pay?"

"I don't know. I'll mention what we discovered to Marshal Jennings. She seems more willing to listen and work with us than her partner."

"At least one of them has an open mind," Sally said.

"Yeah." He frowned. "But other than filling in the marshal, what's our next step?" Sally was so much better at this kind of thing than him. His sole law enforcement experience had been as a military police officer. He had never had to investigate a crime or research anyone during his stint in the military. He never imagined he'd be doing it now either, but the detective in Frank had them all protecting others differently than simply serving as bodyguards.

Sally cleared her throat. "You could see if the judge will pull some strings. Or I can keep digging."

"How about we do both." He stood. "Text me with whatever else you can find out about Hannah no matter how insignificant it seems."

"Will do, boss. Before you go, how is Carissa? She's like a ghost lately."

He hesitated. "You know Carissa. She's a trooper." There was no way he would talk about Carissa behind her back, friend or not. He'd learned that lesson the hard way when he'd assumed Frank knew something, and Marc had ended up revealing private information to Frank. "Give her a call sometime. She protects Hannah during business hours. Hannah sticks close to home when the judge is there, so we aren't needed then."

"I'll do that. I talked to her about doing a

teambuilding outing to an escape room and want to get it scheduled."

"Why not set it up with Frank?"

She rolled her eyes. "Have you seen him around either?"

He looked toward his business partner's office. "Yeah. He's pretty busy."

"You think?" Sally shook her head. "I'm glad he brought on Peter, but boy has it been a wild month."

"Hang in there, Sally. Things are bound to slow down sooner or later." If they didn't, they'd be forced to hire a couple more people. They could use a fulltime admin person who excelled with research. Sally said she didn't mind doing research and was good at it, but they all knew her skills were best used in the field.

"I hope you're right, Marc, because we're spread too thin."

He nodded and left. If Sally was concerned, then he suspected they weren't running the company well. He, Frank, and Carissa needed to have another meeting. Sally never complained.

Marc headed out. He'd parked his pickup near the coffee shop. Carissa would be there soon with Hannah, and he wanted to fill her in on what he'd learned.

Carissa spotted Marc's pickup parked in front of Gently Brewed. Her pulse skipped. She missed him so much.

They had some snuggle time on Saturday night while watching the movie at her place, but their weekend had been too busy for socializing.

She accompanied Hannah into the coffee shop and spotted Marc at the counter talking with Rebecca.

Marc turned and caught Carissa's eye. He led the way into the back, entering first. "Wait here until I clear the room." They'd decided after she'd been conked on the head that he would always be there when Hannah reported to work.

A minute later, he opened the door and motioned for them to join him. "How was your day, Hannah?"

"Fine." She glanced over her shoulder toward him as she slipped an apron over her head.

"Just wondering if anything unusual happened or if anyone said anything that concerned you."

She turned. A frown marred her face. "It was a pretty average day, although I gave Makayla a piece of my mind for setting me up with Carson. I thought she knew him well, but apparently not."

"Speaking of knowing someone well—it's come to my attention that you were adopted."

Hannah caught her breath. "Why are you digging into my life?"

Carissa shot Marc a warning look, hoping he'd understand to tread carefully.

"Guarding you indefinitely isn't feasible. We're trying to determine who's behind your trouble."

"Oh. I guess that makes sense."

She brushed at a piece of imaginary lint on her sweater. "Do you know your birth mother?"

"It was a closed adoption." Hannah appeared indifferent.

"How did you come to live with the judge?" Carissa wanted to know if the judge's answer to the same question would match up with Hannah's.

Hannah crossed her arms. "It was part of my scholarship."

Carissa met Marc's gaze. "A scholarship for what?"

"Some random scholarship for an incoming freshman."

"So you applied for it?" Marc asked.

"I guess. I don't know. All I know is that the financial aid office notified me of the scholarship and the housing perk. It was an answer to prayer. My parents didn't have any money saved for college, and I didn't have much set aside. Between living with Alyssa, the scholarship, and what I make working here, my education and expenses are covered."

"That must be a huge burden lifted from you." Now more than ever, Carissa believed Hannah and the judge were related in some way. Sally had sent her a text about her suspicion that their client was the judge's niece. Assuming that was the case, then someone could be using Hannah to get to the judge.

"What's with all the questions?" Hannah looked to Carissa.

Should she tell her what she thought or stay quiet?

Hannah had a right to know, but would it make things worse for the young woman?

"Maybe you should sit down." Marc moved a folding chair beside Hannah.

Fear filled their client's eyes. "What's going on? You're both freaking me out."

"It's nothing bad," Carissa said, "but it might come as a shock."

"Okay. Tell me. What is it?"

Carissa squatted to her eye level. "We believe Judge Potter could be your aunt. Her twin sister gave up a baby girl for adoption the same year you were born."

Hannah shrugged. "That doesn't mean anything. It's a coincidence."

"Perhaps," Marc said. "Or maybe the judge has been following your life and decided to orchestrate a scholarship for you. She could get to know the niece she never knew."

Hannah bit down on her bottom lip. "If what you're saying is true, why wouldn't she tell me who she is?"

Carissa stood and met Marc's gaze.

Marc shook his head. "We don't know, and we won't be able to find out anything for sure without Judge Potter's cooperation. Do you think you could convince her to help?"

"Maybe. If you're right, and I am her niece, what if she doesn't want it known? Besides that, even if she did tell me, there's the non-disclosure agreement."

"You're right, but maybe you could accidently drop a piece of paper near us with the word yes or no on it." Marc stuffed his hands into his back pockets.

Hannah's brow scrunched. "I suppose."

"When you talk to her, point out that your bodyguards think someone could be using you to get to her."

"You really believe that?" Carissa asked.

"I believe it's possible," Marc said.

The door from the front swung open and Rebecca stood there. "I have someplace to be. Will you be much longer?"

Hannah hopped up. "Sorry. On my way."

Carissa positioned herself at the door dividing the back of the shop from the front so she could keep watch.

Rebecca scooted past her and removed her apron then grabbed a large duffel.

"Where're you heading?" Marc asked.

"Remember that audition I had?"

He nodded.

"I got the part. We start filming today. It's only a regional commercial, but I hope it'll be my big break."

"Congratulations!" Marc grinned. "Break a leg."

"Thanks." Rebecca hoisted the duffle bag strap over her shoulder. "See you." She left through the back door into the alley.

Carissa stepped into the front of the coffee shop once Rebecca had left.

Hannah handed her an Americano. "Your usual."

Carissa grinned. "Thanks." She added cream and sugar then sipped the drink as she headed for her typical seat beside the counter where she had a view of the door as well as the dining area.

Marc joined her, holding a bottle of water. "How'd you know the judge was a twin?"

"Sally."

"I see. She got to you fast."

"That's my girl." She brought the cup to her mouth and took another sip. She'd have to lay off this stuff or risk never sleeping again. But right now, it was the only way she stayed awake, since she wasn't sleeping well. She'd finally made an appointment with a counselor. Her first one was this evening.

"What're you thinking about?" Marc took a gulp from the water bottle.

She shrugged. "I'd like to fill Marshal Jennings in on what we found."

"Already did."

"Aren't you the speedy one?" She winked.

"Whatever it takes to find who's behind Hannah's trouble. If it's related to the judge, then the FBI will take over. Nothing against Hannah, but I reek of coffee."

She laughed. "I almost forgot you can't stand the scent."

The door to the shop flew open and a man wearing a ski mask and holding a semi-automatic weapon burst in. "Everyone get down!"

Carissa reached for her pistol.

He fired a wild round. "Don't!" He waved his gun in their direction. "No heroes, or someone will die. I only want the girl."

"No," Hannah cried then turned and ran for the backroom.

The man chased after her.

"Go," Carissa hissed at Marc as she called 9-1-1. Praise God, they were the only ones in the shop.

Marc raced out the front door, presumably to cut them off at the alley.

Carissa reported the incident then drew her weapon and, crouching, headed toward the back room. Empty. Maybe Hannah was hiding. "Hannah? Are you here? It's safe to come out." She waited a moment. No response.

Her pulse thrummed in her ears. She rushed out the door, leading to the alleyway then stopped and looked both ways. Which way would Hannah have run? A white cat darted behind a garbage can. Carissa ran the twenty or so feet toward the nearest sidewalk.

"Let the girl go and get down!" Marc shouted.

Carissa pulled up short, pushing her body against the building. She dipped her head, peering around the corner and spotted Marc with his gun drawn and aimed at the masked man, who held a knife to Hannah's neck.

They were close. She had a clear shot of the man, but she couldn't take it without risking it would go clean through and hit Hannah too. *We need help, Lord.* She spotted a walnut-shell sized piece of broken asphalt, reached down, and picked it up. If it worked for David when he killed Goliath, it could work for her too. Plus, she had years of experience playing as an outfielder in softball.

Lord, please make this work. She crept out of the alley and drew her arm back. She only had one chance. She reached back then thrust her arm forward releasing the rock.

Her weapon hit its mark. The assailant dropped.

"Run, Hannah," Carissa shouted.

Hannah sprinted to Marc and hid behind him. He met Carissa's gaze. "Wow! You have an arm."

Hannah peeked around Marc. "Is he dead?"

"I hope not." Carissa walked toward the masked man. "I have some questions I'd like answered." She squatted and felt for his pulse. Relief coursed through her. "He's alive."

A police cruiser stopped, and Officer Brady along with another male officer approached. Dillon spoke into the radio on his shoulder requesting an ambulance. "What happened?"

Marc explained what happened and how Carissa had struck the would-be kidnapper. "He appears to be knocked out."

Dillon shot Carissa a broad smile. "We could use you on our softball team this summer." He squatted down and pulled the mask off the man. "Do you know him, Hannah?"

She shook her head. "I've never seen him before.

We should call the marshals protecting Alyssa. He said something about the judge. I'm afraid for her."

So this was related to Judge Potter. Carissa looked at Hannah. "What did he say to you?"

"He said the judge would pay dearly for her precious niece. I know you suggested she was my aunt, but until he said that, I didn't believe it."

An ambulance pulled to a stop at the alleyway entrance. Dillon spoke to one of the medics, while the other one attended the would-be abductor.

Carissa sidled up to Marc and Hannah. "Any idea if he was working alone or how he knew about your relationship to the judge?"

"No. But maybe Alyssa will know."

"Good point," Marc said. "Someone needs to let her know what's going on."

"Right." Hannah pulled out her phone and started texting. "If she's in court, she won't respond."

"That's fine." The adrenalin rush from earlier flat-lined. Carissa forced past the exhaustion. "Officer Brady will notify the marshals. Once we're free to go, we'll take you home and stay with you until the judge is home."

"I can't leave the coffee shop. I'm the only one here."

Marc shook his head. "Call your manager and explain what happened. You're not staying here. We'll lock up."

Carissa moved over to Dillon. "Does the guy have ID?"

"Negative."

The medics moved their John Doe onto the gurney and placed him into the ambulance. Dillon's partner climbed in after them.

"We're taking Hannah home. She let the judge know what's going on."

"Good. I'll fill in the marshals and update you when I know something."

"Thanks, Dillon."

"You doing okay, Carissa? It's been pretty intense for you and your team this month." Lines etched across Dillon's forehead.

"I'm fine. Thanks for asking. But I sure could use a break." Which reminded her about her appointment with the counselor this evening. She might need to reschedule.

19

Carissa sat beside Marc in Frank's office. They had all come in early to debrief. "I spoke with Officer Brady last night," she said. "The perpetrator, Rex Sikes, has history with the judge—rather his mother does. Rex first learned of the judge's twin sister from his mother. Apparently, she was a labor and delivery nurse back when Hannah was born. The judge's family was well known and held in high esteem in the community. They kept the baby quiet to avoid scandal."

Marc rolled his eyes. "You've got to be kidding."

"I wish," Carissa said. "To a wealthy and influential family, a child out of wedlock was a scandal so they sent the girls away."

Frank's eyes widened. "Both of the twins were sent away?"

Carissa nodded. "According to the judge—I talked with her too—they were practically inseparable, and it would have caused a lot of questions if only one left town for the summer. Rex's mom connected her patient to the wealthy family and apparently never forgot her."

Marc shook his head. "She could get in big trouble for revealing that information to her son. She broke privacy laws."

Frank leaned forward. "But why was Rex trying to extort money from the judge? It wasn't like she was Hannah's mother."

"True, but according to Officer Brady, he figured the judge for a bigger payday."

Marc scowled. "So his motivation was money, but why graffiti the garage door?"

"To scare the judge. Technically, he didn't do that. He paid a random girl to do it. He didn't know Judge Potter was out of town. Apparently, he had a personal vendetta against the judge because she was responsible for sentencing his brother to life in prison."

"No way," Marc said. "Of all the judges that could have handled that case, it happened to be the judge his mom had dirt on. Well, at least dirt on her sister, but still…"

Carissa didn't understand why he chose to harass poor Hannah. It was as if he took pleasure in it simply because the judge cared about her. He'd be joining his brother in prison soon.

Marc shifted in his seat. "Is Rex the person who paid Carson to take her on a date and drug her?"

Carissa nodded. "He admitted to that right before lawyering up."

Frank leaned back in his seat. "Sounds like there's

already enough to convict. I'm glad this is wrapped up. I want the two of you to take a day and rest. Then it's all hands-on-deck. We have a musician coming to town."

Marc groaned. "Another musician? My ears are still ringing from the last concert."

Carissa chuckled and playfully slugged his shoulder.

Frank grinned. "This one is a classical pianist. I don't think you'll have that problem."

"I'm not a fan, but at least I won't suffer hearing loss." Marc rested his ankle on his knee. "Anything else going on?"

"Do you remember Jenna Walsh?"

Carissa nodded. "Of course. I thought she released us."

"She did, but Peter has a soft spot for her and doesn't think she's safe. I encouraged him to help her out pro-bono while I try and figure out who's behind those notes she received. Her dad is a good man and got a raw deal because of her situation. I'd like to see justice done, regardless of the money."

Frank took on pet projects so this came as no surprise. "That's fine, but we need Peter working for us too." They hired him for a reason—they needed him.

"Don't worry," Frank said. "He understands. The fact that he's willing to donate his time to protecting Jenna says a lot about his character. I'm glad we hired him."

Marc stood. "Agreed. We'll see you tomorrow night."

Carissa grabbed her purse from beside her feet and joined Marc. "Let's get out of here before we get sucked into work again."

Frank chuckled. "You know you love it."

Marc guffawed. "That's the problem. She's going to work herself into an early grave." Marc draped his arm across her shoulder as they strolled out.

Carissa loved her job, and the men she worked with were the best, but she needed a day off to recuperate after yesterday. A day with nothing to do but read a good book. "What do you say we pick up coffee and hang out at my place today?"

"Minus the coffee I like the sound of that."

She chuckled. "We can skip coffee today."

"Seriously?" He tipped his head and stared into her eyes. "I think that conk on the head you took a while back is having a delayed effect."

"Very funny." Though she wasn't ready to say the words, true love was the reason she was willing to skip the coffee shop today. He'd figure it out sooner or later.

"What's that smile about?"

"That's for me to know and you to find out—someday."

"Intriguing."

Today was going to be fun.

20

Thursday evening, Jenna sat on her sofa with a book, but the words all blurred together. She closed it and set it aside. What did people who didn't work fifty-plus hours a week do? She wasn't accustomed to free time. Too bad Peter was still gone—she missed him.

Their last conversation had been simmering in her mind since Monday. She knew he was a Christian, but the man really lived it and wasn't afraid to be real. That wasn't something she'd witnessed all that often.

"Lord, I want the kind of peace that Peter seems to have. I know I need to let go of the anger, but it's so hard. It's not fair what happened to my parents. To be honest, I don't even want to go to church anymore. I know it was a small group of loud people who caused the problem and that I shouldn't blame the entire church for the actions of a select few. But again, I'm so angry. Why is this happening to my parents? I'm sorry for letting my temper get the best of me and causing all this to begin with."

Trust Me.

Sudden tears pooled in her eyes as a warm sensation filled her. She moved to the kitchen, added water to a mug, then placed it in the microwave. She reached for the box with hot chocolate envelopes and tore off the top. The microwave beeped, and she finished making her drink. She couldn't shake the sense that the Lord had told her to trust Him.

She stilled. Would trusting Him take the anger away? Those people didn't deserve her forgiveness. She leaned against the counter and sipped the sweet treat. A sermon her dad gave years ago played in her mind.

All have sinned and fall short—none of us is deserving of forgiveness, but it's a free gift, paid for by Jesus. She shook her head, flicking the thoughts away. A knock sounded on her door. Who could that be? Maybe Peter was back. Her insides fluttered, and she rushed to the door and swung it open. "Mom. What are you doing here?"

Mom stepped in with a chuckle. "Is that how you greet all your guests?"

Jenna frowned and closed the door. "Would you like something to drink? I have hot chocolate." She still held her mug.

"That sounds nice, thanks." Mom stood and looked around her apartment. "It's a far cry from your old place, but I like it. It's homey. You did a nice job."

Jenna froze. "Really?" Her mom had a critical eye when it came to home design and décor. She counted it a huge win to have her mother's approval. "It's vintage."

211

"There's nothing wrong with that." She sat on the sofa.

Jenna moved to the kitchen and prepared hot chocolate for her mom then brought it to her and sat on the other end. "It's comfortable but a little shabby."

Mom sipped her drink then placed it on a coaster on the coffee table. "If you ever want to reupholster it, let me know. I've been itching to try my hand at that."

"You'd want to help?"

"Absolutely. Can you imagine this in soft blue velvet? Wouldn't that be beautiful?"

Jenna nodded. "That sounds beautiful, and I'd love your help." What had come over her mom? Maybe Dad's retirement had been the best thing that came out of that viral video. "What brings you by?"

"I wanted to see how you're doing?"

Mom never came over. There had to be more to it. "You could've called."

Mom grinned. "But then I wouldn't have gotten to see your apartment. I'm really proud of how you came through the storm."

Jenna laughed drily. "You mean my life?"

Mom nodded. "I know it was rough, and you're still working on things, but I'm truly impressed by your attitude change and what you've accomplished." She sipped her hot chocolate.

"Thanks."

"Based on how this place looks, I feel like I already know the answer to this, but I'll ask anyway. How are you? I know your dad and I sprung some pretty unsettling news on you."

"I'm still processing." Should she tell Mom how angry she was? Would she be disappointed in her? "May I ask you something?"

"Of course." Mom rested her mug on her lap, cradled between her hands.

"How come you're so happy?"

"I didn't realize I was. Perhaps you're actually wondering why I'm not upset about the situation with your dad?"

"Maybe that's a better way to put it, but you *are* happy. I don't remember the last time you stopped by like this." Her face heated. "You're being so nice."

Mom blushed. "I suppose I've often been hard on you, but I felt the need to balance your Dad's indulgences with you."

After overhearing their argument that night, she knew the truth of her mother's words.

"I'll be completely honest. I was furious at first. I'm embarrassed by my behavior now. After I calmed down and prayed, I realized this is actually a good thing for your dad and me. He never would have retired, and it was time. He's ready for a new chapter in his life."

"Sure, but what they did was wrong." She really needed to let this go and stop harping on it, but she couldn't.

"I agree. Remember, the Lord can use bad for good."

"True." Is that why Mom was so calm and at peace? "Regardless of the good that's come from it, I'm still working through my anger."

"I was afraid of that. I don't want you to blame yourself, Jenna. I believe those people were looking for a way to force your dad out and would have eventually succeeded with or without that video."

A tiny bit of guilt fell away.

"I have a gift for you out in my car."

"Really? What is it?"

"You'll see." Mom stood. "I wasn't sure it'd go, so I didn't want to bring it up with me until I saw your place. Be right back."

"Do you need help?"

"Nope." She grinned and went outside.

A few minutes later, Mom walked in carrying a watercolor about the size of a vinyl record jacket. The autumn colors played nicely with her thrift store finds.

Tears burned the backs of Jenna's eyes as she struggled to find her voice without full-on crying. Her mom had never painted anything for her. "It's beautiful. Thank you." She took the art and placed it on the kitchen counter then hugged her mom. "I love you."

"I love you too." She cleared her throat. "I don't want to overstay my welcome. I should go. I have a stop to make before going home."

"Okay. Thanks for coming over." Surprise filled her at the realization she truly meant those words. She wasn't super close to her mom, but tonight felt like a new beginning. Jenna walked her to the door.

"Would you like to come over for Sunday dinner?" Mom asked.

"Sure. Can I bring a friend if he's free?"

"He?" Mom raised a brow.

Jenna shook her head and waved a hand. "He's my neighbor, and the man who was watching out for me after those notes came. He works for Frank, the guy Dad recommended."

The light in Mom's eyes faded ever so slightly. "Oh, I see. Sure. He's welcome to join us. See you Sunday." She turned and left.

Smiling, Jenna closed and locked the door then took their mugs to the kitchen and loaded them into the dishwasher. Funny how one short visit with her mom changed her entire outlook. True joy filled her.

A scraping sound against her door drew her attention. She dried her hands then walked over to the door and pulled it open. "Did you forget…?" No one was there. She looked right then left. No one. She looked down and saw a piece of paper. Her heart thudded. *Not again.*

Peter stood stage right while Tom Iotta performed *Beethoven's Fifth Symphony* on the piano. Unease skirted through him. Every concert this week had gone off without a hitch. Would tonight be the exception?

They were all on high alert for their client's final concert in Seattle. Frank stood stage left scanning the audience for trouble, and Marc and Carissa stood near exits. Sally was on call in case they needed her. He prayed they wouldn't.

Too bad Jenna wasn't here. She would probably enjoy this concert. Tom had a gift, and the concertgoers had seemed to really appreciate his performances. On second thought, their client could be in danger, so he was glad Jenna wasn't here. He didn't want her anywhere near possible trouble.

He sure missed her though. She'd been much more fun to protect. To be fair though, the moody and quiet musician had been relatively easy to deal with the past few days. He prayed things would continue as normal like they had each concert before this one.

Peter looked toward the audience. Everyone appeared mesmerized by the musician, but he couldn't shake the sense that something wasn't right.

The piano reached a crescendo. A loud boom punctuated the air. He dropped to the floor. Smoke filtered in from the lobby. Tom stopped playing and turned toward him with fear-filled eyes.

Peter stood and ran in a crouched position across the stage. He took Tom's arm. "Let's go."

Tom's arm shook beneath his grip.

Frank ran over to him. Together they created a human shield for Tom. "I've called 9-1-1. Get him back to his hotel. I'll meet you there as soon as possible." He escorted them behind the stage and to the exit. "I'll have Sally check the room before you arrive. The hotel security's been alerted as well. They'll meet you at the kitchen entrance."

Peter nodded. He knew the contingency plan by heart. They'd planned for this very situation.

To his credit, Tom stayed quiet and cooperative.

Keeping an eye on their surroundings, Peter escorted Tom to the rented Sedan. Their intel hadn't indicated a bomb threat. If he had to guess, he'd say at least one pipe bomb had exploded. Was it connected to his client or was it a random act of violence? The police would have to figure that out.

Peter checked under the sedan for a bomb then secured Tom in the vehicle and merged into traffic. Emergency vehicles en route to the concert hall sped toward them. He checked his mirrors. No one appeared to be following them. He made a few evasive maneuvers—still no one. His grip on the steering wheel eased.

Would this incident force Tom to extend his time in Seattle while the police investigated?

A short while later, Peter pulled up to the hotel's kitchen entrance where two security guards stood.

"Stay put." Peter got out of the car and walked over to the guards. "I'm Peter King."

The larger of the two men nodded. "We're here to escort Mr. Iotta to his room."

Peter confirmed their identities then nodded. He

scanned the area then opened the door for his client. "These men will escort you to your room. Sally is there. I'll be up soon."

Tom nodded. "Thank you. I'll see you shortly."

Peter wondered at the man's sudden wordiness since he'd barely spoken more than two words at a time all week. It had been a *long* week. He slid behind the wheel then headed for the underground parking lot. Thankfully, there was a spot near the elevators.

A short while later Peter rapped their special knock on the door, and Sally admitted him. The serious look on her face said it all. Their client was in trouble if they couldn't find and stop the bomber. "You made good time. Was the room clear?"

"Yeah." Sally stepped aside, allowing him to enter. "I was close. You good on your own? I have a date with my pillow."

He nodded. "Sleep well." At least one of them should. Hopefully, the authorities would be by to collect their statements in the not-too-distant future, and Tom would be able to catch the last flight out of Seattle as planned. He shot off a text to Frank asking for him to expedite things if possible.

He turned to Tom. "Who did you cross?"

Tom's shoulders slumped as he sank onto the apartment-sized couch. He propped his elbow on his knees and rested his head in his hands. "If I thought for one minute speaking out in support of that woman would've caused all this trouble, I never would have. Do you think anyone was hurt at the concert?"

"I don't know. I'll try and find out, but in the meantime, how about you tell me about the woman?" A sinking feeling gripped him as he sent a text to Frank inquiring about casualties.

No casualties.

Peter blew out a breath. "Everyone is okay."

The tension on Tom's face eased slightly. "Good. The woman's name is Jenna. She worked for an ad company I once did business with. She did an excellent job, and I've been following her work ever since. According to the video I saw, Kratt Paper is up to no good. The trolls online were having a field day at her expense, and I simply spoke up in her defense during an interview with a local radio station. I never intended to speak on her behalf, but the DJ had asked me a question, and I used her situation as an example."

"An example of what?"

"The dangers of big corporations having too much power."

"Why would they ask *you* a question like that? You play the piano for a living."

He shrugged. "I've been known to stand up for the small business man. Apparently, the DJ had seen an old interview I'd done."

"I had no idea." Nor did he know the man could string together so many words. It turned out their client had a voice and knew how to use it.

"Anyway," Tom said, "after seeing the video, I did some research and discovered that what Jenna said was, in all likelihood, true. I also made the mistake of mentioning the name of the company. It's been a nightmare ever since."

Why hadn't Frank filled him in on this key detail? Maybe he hadn't known, considering how tight-lipped their client had been up to now. "Have you received any threats or anything that caused you alarm before that interview?" Peter crossed his arms and leaned against a high counter. This case had taken an unexpected turn. How many others were being intimidated, and more specifically, who was behind it?

"No. That's why I hired you. Since then, there've been multiple threats online, and then last week, a letter came in the mail to my home in Dallas, Texas."

"Did you show Frank that letter?"

He frowned and his face reddened. "I set it on the coffee table, and my dog ate it."

Peter blinked. "Excuse me?"

"I know what it sounds like, but my dog is still a puppy and eats anything she can get her mouth on. I should've put it up higher, but I was so shocked, I dropped it on the table, and the next thing I knew Paige had it in her mouth. I tried to get it away from her, but—"

"I get the picture." Peter pulled out his phone and scrolled until he found a picture of Jenna's most recent letter. "Did it look anything like this?"

Tom looked at the note. He jerked his head up and met Peter's gaze. "Where did you get this?"

"Another client received it."

"Mine used cut out letters too."

"What did it say?"

"You talk too much. Now you'll pay."

"Stay put, Tom. I'm going to step outside your room and make a call." He had to reach Jenna. The phone rang twice.

"Peter?" Fear tinged her voice.

"Yes. Are you okay?"

"Not really. I received another letter a little bit ago."

"What'd it say?"

"Time is running out."

What was that supposed to mean? "Is that all it said?" He ran a hand along the back of his neck, kneading the tight muscles.

"Yes."

"Any idea what it means?"

"None, but my imagination is running wild. What should I do?"

"I'm tied up with my client for the night, or I'd come over. Can you stay with your parents?"

"My mom left here right before the letter came. Peter, I think whoever's doing this is watching me. If I leave, they'll follow."

He had a feeling she was right. He'd ask Carissa to stay with her but quickly tossed the thought aside. Sally made more sense since Jenna knew her better. "Are you okay with me asking Sally to come over?"

"I discontinued my contract with Protection Inc., remember?"

"I realize that. I'd have to clear it through Frank first, but I'm sure my team will agree you shouldn't be alone."

"No. I don't want you to ask anyone to come over. I don't think whoever left this note is going to do anything more tonight. I'll be okay. It just freaked me out. Hearing your voice helped me calm down. Why'd you call?"

How much could he tell her? Peter shook his head. It would be all over the media soon if it wasn't already. He told her about the bomb and how his client had stood up for her during his radio interview.

"Oh no! Now I feel even worse. Because of me, lives are at stake. I had no idea how far reaching this was."

"Don't blame yourself, Jenna. You're not responsible for the actions of others."

"But if it wasn't for me—"

"Don't go there."

"I have to go there. It's my fault." Her voice caught.

He ached to hold her and tell her everything would be okay, but he knew better than to promise something he couldn't guarantee. "Hang in there. We're doing everything we can. Like it or not the police are involved now."

"I know it's for the best." She sighed. "I hate what's going on."

"We all do. Try to sleep. I'll check in with you tomorrow. Good night." He walked back into the hotel room and stopped mid-step. "What happened? You look like you've seen a ghost."

Tom held up a piece of paper.

21

Friday night Jenna sat in her apartment with heaviness on her like she'd never experienced before. She had called in sick to work after having stayed awake all night. Besides, she didn't want to put Brandi in any danger. Peter had sent a text stating that no one had been injured in the blast, but she still couldn't shake that she'd set things in motion, and people could potentially have been injured.

A rap on her door made her jump. She stood and approached it with caution. "Who is it?"

"Peter."

She jerked the door wide and flung herself at him, wrapping her arms around his neck.

His arms enveloped her, making her feel safe for the first time since she'd learned of the bombing last night. He rubbed her back and spoke softly. "How about we get out of the doorway?"

She caught her breath and dropped her arms to her sides. "Sorry. I didn't mean to throw myself at you like that." She stepped back.

He chuckled as he moved into her apartment and closed the door behind him. "You can greet me like that anytime you'd like." He winked.

"Oh stop." She playfully punched his arm, not in the least bit upset by his words. Was he feeling as drawn to her as she was to him? "What are you doing here?"

"My client returned home. He felt he was safer there, and we all agreed after he discovered a note along with a photograph of him stuffed in his bathrobe pocket. It had an X marked through his face."

Her eyes widened. "Someone was in his room? And they went through his stuff." She shivered. Thank God that hadn't happened to her.

"Yes. He discovered it while I was on the phone with you last night. After giving a statement to the police regarding the situation, he couldn't escape Seattle fast enough. Frank has a contact in Dallas that will take care of our client there."

"Wow. It's all so surreal." She shook her head. "Come have a seat. I'll make us hot chocolate."

"Thanks." He instead followed her to the kitchen and leaned against the counter as she heated the water. "As I stated last night, the police are now involved. Frank felt it prudent to fill them in on your case."

Fear gripped her. Somehow having the police involved upped the seriousness of the situation. "I understand." Though she had hoped to keep her involvement quiet, bringing in the authorities was the right thing to do at this point, considering how things had escalated.

Peter moved close to her and ducked down until their gazes met. "You okay?" He reached for her hand and held it lightly between them.

"Not really." Her voice caught. She cleared her throat, willing her wrung-out emotions to settle down. "I don't like admitting it, but I'm scared."

He pulled her into a hug. "I'm here now, and I won't let anything happen to you." His chin rested lightly on the top of her head.

She relaxed against him. This felt good—too good. They couldn't let their guards down right now. Not until the note sender was found and in custody. She gently eased back from him until his arms dropped to his sides. "Thanks. A hug always makes me feel better."

The serious look on his face relaxed. "I'm glad to help."

She placed several heaping teaspoons of hot chocolate mix into the mugs and poured hot water over the powdery mound in the bottom. The aroma eased her tension. She added a spoon and handed Peter his mug. "Let's sit in the other room." She moved to the couch and sat.

Peter stopped and looked at her mom's artwork on the wall. "I don't remember seeing this before."

"It's new. My mom painted it."

"She's good." He joined her on the couch, choosing the middle spot on the three-cushion sofa. "Do you have the letter you received last night?"

"Let's enjoy this first." She needed a few more

minutes of reprieve. "I've missed you."

"Same here. More than I care to admit."

Was Peter blushing? She brought her mug to her lips, hiding her grin.

"How's work?" Peter sipped his cocoa.

"Great. But I didn't go today. I was awake all night. When I explained my night to Brandi, she suggested I stay home."

He winced. "Now I wish I hadn't told you what happened. I'm sorry you lost sleep."

She reached for his hand. A tingle zipped up her arm. Oh boy, she was in trouble. She liked Peter way too much. "I'm glad you called. I would've been up all night anyway because of the letter I received." With a sigh, she let go of his hand and stood. Might as well get it over with. She retrieved the item that had caused her anxiety. She'd placed it into a clear plastic bag to protect it. "Here you go."

"Thanks." Peter held up the bag and looked at the letter. "'Time is running out.' I wonder what it means."

"I took it as a death threat."

His gaze slammed into hers. "That's certainly one way to look at it."

"Can you think of another?" To her way of thinking, that was the only interpretation for a message like that.

"Time is running out might be in reference to anything. It could have been about the bombing last night. Or refer to something even bigger that he's planning, or even his timetable—maybe he's almost done harassing you."

"Do you really believe that?" She eyed him. He was probably trying to make her feel less afraid.

"No. I believe this is a warning of something big to come. What that is I don't know, but it's not necessarily a death threat."

"I think your client had the right idea about getting out of Seattle. I have a cousin in California. Maybe I should go for an extended visit."

He frowned. "That's an option."

"But not one you like."

"I can't protect you if you're in California."

"I might not need protecting there."

"It's your call, but I think it's an unnecessary risk. I'd feel much better if you stayed here."

She looked down then back at him and sighed. "I can't leave anyway. I have a new job and rent to pay. I don't want to lose either. I kind of like it here." She forced a grin.

He tugged her to his side, resting an arm across the back of the couch and grazing her neck. "I'm glad. I like you being here. I like having you as a neighbor too."

"An incredibly needy one though."

"You're not that bad. After all, you give me pizza and hot chocolate." He raised his mug.

Somehow, he always managed to make her feel better.

Worry ate at Peter as he sat beside Jenna. Were it not for his concern for her, he'd be at home, sound asleep. His body ached from lack of rest, but whoever was sending these letters wasn't messing around anymore, and Jenna couldn't be left alone. The two pipe bombs that went off at the concert hall last night were evidence enough.

"Peter?"

"Hmm?"

"I'm scared."

He set his mug on a coaster then took her hand with his free one. "Frank is tenacious. He'll figure out who's behind this and stop them. Plus, the police are working on finding the bomber."

"But will they find him before it's too late? And what if we're talking about two different people?"

"I don't know, Jenna. But realize this: I won't let anything happen to you." The letters on the note were imprinted on his mind. *Time is running out.* Never before had he felt such an urgency to solve a case. "How about if I make myself a fixture in your life until this guy gets caught? I have the next couple of days off, so my time is my own."

"It sounds nice, but I can't ask you to do that without paying you, and I don't have that kind of money."

He blew out a breath. Didn't she realize he wanted

to be there for her, paid or not? "Don't insult me. You have to know by now that I care about you. I don't want anything to happen to you, and I'm more than happy to spend my off-time keeping you safe."

Her eyes widened. "Okay. Thank you."

"If things escalate, I know the entire team would step in to help regardless of pay. That's how they are. They care about people."

"I won't let the entire company donate their time to me." She shook her head. "But I appreciate that they'd be willing. I feel a little guilty about you working on your days off for no pay."

He had a nice nest egg and lived below his means. "I wouldn't offer if I didn't want to do this for you. Plus, I'm not losing any money. Like I said, I'm off for a couple of days." He caressed her hand with his thumb. "Please let me do this for you. Don't feel guilty. I wouldn't be able to rest knowing you didn't have someone looking out for you. So you're really doing me a favor."

She chuckled. "You win."

"Thank you."

She tilted her head to the side. "How is this going to work if I need protection beyond the weekend? I have a job. You can't hang out in that tiny office all day."

"I say we enjoy the weekend, and let Monday worry about itself." He tried to keep his voice light. Jenna was scared enough. She didn't need to know how concerned he was for her. Protection Inc. had had three clients recently with one thing in common—Jenna's video. Frank was determined to find the person behind all the trouble. He was not going to let this drop. Based on what he had observed of the man, Frank could have the person's identity figured out by Monday.

"What do you say we explore the city tomorrow? I've only been here a short time, and I've heard about all sorts of interesting things I'd like to see."

"Sure. What do you have in mind? There's the Space Needle, the waterfront, the Fremont Troll, the aquarium, the locks—"

"You choose. It all sounds good to me." Maybe planning their day tomorrow would keep her mind off her trouble.

"What kind of stuff do you like? There really is a ton to see and do here. Way more than I said."

"I'm easy. Just don't tell anyone where we're going."

Her body stiffened. "So don't make any reservations or buy tickets to anything in advance, that kind of thing?"

"You catch on fast." He caressed her hand with his thumb. "When this is all over, I'll make us dinner reservations to wherever you'd like."

She raised a brow. "That sounds like a date."

"Are you okay with that?" Had he assumed too much? Did she only see him as a friendly neighbor and protector?

A slow smile spread across her face. "I am. I can't wait."

He released the breath he'd been holding. "Me either. The sooner this guy is behind bars the better."

Her brow furrowed. "Is that the only reason you can't wait?"

Either she was blind or playing coy. He released her hand and tipped up her chin with his finger. "One of several," he said softly. His gaze searched hers. He saw trust and desire. He lowered his mouth and brushed her lips with his.

A knock sounded on the door in a unique but familiar pattern.

Jenna jumped away, her eyes wide. "Who could that be at this time of night?"

"That would be Sally. I forgot to mention she'll be bunking with you until we find this guy."

Her lips formed an O. "Why didn't you say something sooner?" She stood and rushed to the door.

He beat her there and stopped her before she could open it. "Never open the door without asking first who it is."

"But you said it's Sally."

"Doesn't matter. Confirm."

She rolled her eyes. "Who's there?"

"Sally."

She shot him a saucy look. "Satisfied?"

He chuckled. "Thank you."

She pulled open the door, and his co-worker walked inside.

"Hi, Sally. I'm sorry, I'm not prepared." Jenna shot him a look of annoyance then turned her focus back to his co-worker. "Peter neglected to tell me you were coming until you arrived."

Sally waved a hand. "Not to worry. I have everything I need." She patted a large duffel bag. "Do you mind if I set up my mattress?"

Jenna motioned at the duffel. "You have a mattress in there?"

Sally nodded. "It's an inflatable single bed."

"Cool. Set it up wherever you'd like. I'll give you the grand tour when you're ready."

"I'll be going," Peter said. "If you need anything, I'm right next door."

"We know," Sally said. "Go home and sleep. I heard you were up all night."

He'd been awake for over twenty-four hours. "You heard correctly. See you in the morning."

Jenna moved to open the door for him. "Good night," she said softly.

He forced his hands to stay at his sides and left. Jenna had no idea how she had changed everything. He wasn't sure when it'd happened either. He had been determined to avoid a relationship, and here he was in the same place he'd been a year ago. Was he making a mistake?

Jenna turned back to face Sally, who watched her closely. How was she supposed to act normal after Peter's kiss? Her heart still raced. Could Sally tell? She glanced toward the woman who seemed to know something was up, but not what. *Whew.* Things with Peter were too new and uncertain to share with anyone. "How about that tour?"

"Sounds good." Sally dropped the mattress onto the living room floor.

"It'll be a short tour." Jenna walked to the hall. "The shared bathroom is on the left, and my room is on the right. You'll find extra towels and washcloths under the bathroom sink. If you need anything, ask. I don't have a lot here, but if I have it, consider it fair game."

"Thanks." Sally turned and went back to the living room. She pulled out a black battery-operated pump and attached it to the deflated mattress. "This will only take a few minutes. Hopefully, your neighbors won't mind the noise." Sally flipped the switch and the pump roared to life. A few minutes later, she shut it off then covered the mattress with a fitted sheet and a blanket.

"Do you need a pillow?"

Sally pulled out a travel size pillow and held it up. "No need to stay up for me. You look like the walking dead. Go get some beauty sleep."

Jenna had half a mind to feel offended, but the woman came to protect her. "I will. Thanks for being here. Good night, Sally."

"'Night."

Jenna double-checked the lock on the door then headed to her room. Peter's kiss had certainly surprised her tonight. Sally's timing had been the worst. Then again, maybe it'd been perfect. She touched a finger to her lips. No way would she be sleeping anytime soon.

A rap on her bedroom door drew her attention. "Come in."

Sally opened the door, holding a piece of paper. "This just arrived. I heard a rustling at your front door and when I investigated, I found an envelope."

"Not again." Jenna took the paper from the envelope and read it. "Tick tock." She flipped over the paper. "That's it?" She sucked in a sharp breath. Her pulse beat wildly. "I'm afraid something big and bad is going to happen before this person is caught."

"You could be right, but I've worked for Frank for a couple of months, and since I've been with Protection Inc., he's had a flawless track record. Don't count him out." She motioned toward the letter. "I tried to find the person who left it, but they were too quick." She frowned. "It's almost as if they ducked into one of the other apartments. I don't understand how they vanished so fast."

"I don't like the sound of that at all." She shivered. "Do you mind talking through all of this with me?"

"If you think it will help you sleep."

"All I know is that I won't sleep without talking first."

Sally nodded and headed back to the living room.

Jenna followed and plopped onto the couch.

Sally settled onto her mattress, looking decidedly comfortable. "Do you know if there are surveillance cameras in your apartment complex?"

"The only ones I know of are in the common areas. You'll have to ask Peter though. I know he checked into it."

Sally nodded. "I'll do that first thing tomorrow. I don't want to bother him in case he's sleeping already. What are your thoughts about your case?"

Relief poured through Jenna. She did not want to talk about Peter. "I've been taking these notes as a personal threat. They started after the video went viral. What if we've been looking at this all wrong? What if the person is really on my side, or rather the side of the environment, and isn't sending me a personal threat but rather a warning that if something isn't done soon, the paper company will continue to do irreparable damage?"

Sally pursed her lips and sat up. "It's an interesting idea, especially since someone tried to kill the chairman of the board at Kratt Paper. The police caught and arrested the guy, but I suppose he could've been hired. The police thought he was acting on his own so…"

Which probably ruled out that theory.

"The note left in our client's hotel room was very much a personal threat. It had nothing to do with the paper company and everything to do with him."

"Maybe they aren't connected." Jenna wanted

answers but it appeared that wasn't to be—at least for now.

"Maybe not directly, but indirectly for sure. His notes were made of cut-out letters like yours."

"So? It's not exactly a unique method. Anyone who's ever watched a movie or television would have seen it done. Maybe there are two people out there acting on their own."

"Again, possible, but not probable," Sally said. "I'll definitely run your theory by the team, but you still need to be vigilant and watch your back."

Jenna nodded. But no matter who watched her back, they couldn't stop a bomb if they didn't know about it. Thankfully, no lives were lost in the bombing last night. She couldn't help wonder what the person would do next. She shivered at the thought.

22

After a long day of sightseeing, Peter was ready to put his feet up. He grasped Jenna's hand as they left the monorail and headed for his car. "What do you say we get takeout then head home?"

"Sounds good to me. I didn't realize how tiring playing tourist could be."

"No kidding, but I do feel like I know the city better, and it was fun to see things I'd only read about." They'd walked almost all day, starting at Seattle Center and ending on the waterfront. The uphill trek back had been a killer. Thankfully, Jenna thought to use the monorail and probably saved him a few blisters on his feet.

"Was it spontaneous enough?"

He chuckled. "Considering we were completely impulsive about the streets we chose to walk on, I'd say so." There was no way the person sending those notes would have been able to predict their itinerary since they didn't even know what they were going to do until they did it.

Jenna stopped beside the passenger door of his SUV. "Let's get some food. I'm starving. You in the mood for Chinese?"

Peter opened the door for her. "I happen to know a great place that's on our way." When he got behind the steering wheel, he started the engine and left the parking lot. A few minutes later, he glanced in his rearview mirror and frowned. A compact red car had stayed exactly two cars behind them since they left the parking lot. He sped through a yellow light and watched to see what the car would do.

It swerved around the vehicles and started to run the light but slid to a stop when traffic crossed in front of him.

"Everything okay?" Concern edged Jenna's voice.

"We were being followed."

She turned and looked behind them. "Did you see the driver?"

"No. He was a couple of cars behind me." He shouldn't have tried to elude him so fast. Maybe he could have maneuvered it so the car came close enough for him to get a look at the driver, but all he thought of in the moment was losing him. He made a quick right and then another. With any luck he'd be able to follow their tail.

"Where're we going? I thought you said this place was on the way."

"We're taking a slight detour. I want to try and get the plate number of the car that was following us."

"Oh. Great idea." She pulled out her cell phone.

"I'll take a picture."

He nodded, rounded the next corner, and slipped into traffic heading in the direction they'd been going. "Do you see any small red cars?" It looked as though they'd lost him. Unless... He glanced in his rearview mirror. "Gotcha." The red car must have followed them around the block—short light. "He's behind the car behind us. I'm going to slow to encourage the person between us to pass, then you take a picture of the car through our back window."

"Okay." Jenna said, her voice quavering. "I'll try to get a decent picture."

He pressed the brake, slowing to a little below the speed limit. The car behind him signaled and moved in beside them. Peter slowed a bit more. "Get ready."

Jenna shifted and twisted to face behind them. She held out her camera. "Got it. I couldn't really see the person behind the wheel. He's wearing a baseball cap and sunglasses, but I think I got a good pic of the car." She twisted back around, secured her seatbelt, then viewed the picture on her phone. The car looked familiar. But there had to be thousands like it driving around Seattle.

He glanced at the phone in her lap. "Will you text that to me and e-mail it to Frank?"

"On it." Her thumbs flew across the keypad. "Done. Now what?"

"Now we lose him for good this time."

"How? He knows where we live?"

"We aren't going there after all. One of the reasons

240

I applied for the job at Protection Inc. is because I inherited a property up in Warm Beach several years ago. It's a nice out-of-the-way retreat."

"Really? How did you get so lucky?"

"Luck had nothing to do with it. My favorite aunt, who had a large part in raising me, left it to me when she passed away. I spent many summers and holidays at her place when I was younger."

"I'm sorry."

"It's okay." They said time heals all wounds, but he would forever miss Aunt Charlotte.

"I have to work on Monday," Jenna warned.

"I'm aware. We finally have a lead. Pray."

Jenna closed her eyes as she sat beside Peter in his SUV. *Lord, please help Frank catch this guy before he hurts someone.* "I mentioned this idea to Sally last night, and I'd like to run it by you." She explained her theory that the letter writer could actually support her stand against Kratt Paper and had something big planned against them. Another thought hit her. "What if he's doing something he knows is wrong, and in his own odd or sick way, he's trying to get me to stop him before it's too late?"

"How do you figure? The early notes in no way indicated that. You were called a traitor and a liar in one of them."

She bit her bottom lip. "Good point. Maybe he had

a change of heart."

Peter shook his head. "No. That doesn't make sense. What does make sense is that he has something big planned, and he's toying with you. He wants to scare you. Let you know he's aware of where you are and something is going to happen soon."

Jenna's body quavered. She stiffened, trying to stop the shakes. As much as she appreciated Peter's honesty and frankness, she much preferred her own theory.

"You okay?" Peter glanced her way with sympathy-filled eyes.

"No. I'm scared."

"I know, but we're going to catch this guy."

"Speaking of, have you lost him yet?"

"Miles ago. We'll stop at a place near Warm Beach for necessities before heading to the house."

"How long has it been since you were there?"

"A year or so."

She wrinkled her adorable nose. "It's probably covered in dust."

"I have a housekeeper come in once a month to dust and do general cleaning. I like the idea of someone checking in on the place since I can't."

"Smart." He'd thought of everything except a chaperone—not that they needed one, but the idea of staying alone with him knotted her stomach. She took a breath and let it out slowly. Her parents would agree with this decision even if they'd raised her to not spend the night alone in the same house with a man. Which reminded her, they had dinner plans with her parents tomorrow night. Hopefully, they'd still make it. She couldn't wait for her parents to meet Peter. She knew they'd like him.

He was the perfect gentleman. In fact, he'd only held her hand a few times all day. She had hoped he'd repeat their kiss from last night, but so far nothing. Keeping things casual was probably for the best. They both had a lot going on. The last thing either of them needed was a relationship to distract them from finding and catching whoever was behind the notes and the bombs. But she looked forward to when there were no obstacles in their way.

"You're quiet. What are you thinking about?"

"You, me, and the creep who's messing with me." She might as well voice her thoughts; she wasn't one to tap dance around difficult topics. "I think we need to put us in time out."

"Us?" Surprise lit his voice.

Her face heated. "I mean…uh. You kissed me last night. I thought you were interested. I know I am." She shook her head. "Forget it."

He chuckled. "I'm sorry. I didn't mean to embarrass or fluster you, and I didn't forget kissing you. I simply hadn't taken us beyond that in my mind."

"Oh," her voice fell flat in the quiet of the vehicle. Even though there wasn't technically anything more than a good friendship between them, she'd hoped for more. "So you aren't interested?" He'd said he cared about her. Had she misinterpreted his meaning?

"I never said that. But I do agree with you. We need to focus on keeping you safe."

She cleared her throat. "Good. I'm glad we agree." She should have kept her mouth shut. Apparently, she would never learn when to zip her lips. "Let's solve this thing."

"You and me?" Surprise filled his voice.

"Why not?"

"For starters, we aren't detectives."

"So what? That doesn't mean we can't follow the evidence." The Lord knew who was behind this. "We need to pray for guidance and wisdom."

"I agree." He glanced her way as he signaled and pulled off the freeway. "We'll do our shopping here. The selection near my house isn't great." A few minutes later he pulled into a grocery store parking lot. "Let's pick up enough food for the weekend then figure this out."

She grinned. "Now you're talking." She glanced at the large grocery store that looked like a one-stop-shopping kind of place. Maybe they'd have a T-shirt she could buy to sleep in tonight.

They got out and found provisions. She even scored a pair of sweats to go with the T-shirt as well as a few personal items and favorite snack foods. She brought her bounty to the register and paid then waited for Peter to finish.

"Looks like you did well." Peter paid for his

selections then pulled out his keys as they strode for the exit.

She grinned, thankful her automatic deposit paycheck made it to her account yesterday.

Thirty minutes later, they pulled into a long driveway that wound through giant fir trees. They came to a clearing in front of a modest, white, single-level ranch-style house.

"Home sweet home for the next twenty-four hours." Peter put his SUV in park and got out.

Jenna grabbed her bag and met him at the front door. "It looks nice."

"Thanks. It's nothing fancy. Most importantly, no one followed us. You'll be safe here."

"Good. We need to focus on figuring out who the letter sender is." She was tired of this game of cat and mouse.

Peter unlocked the door and pushed it open. "After you."

She stepped inside the home that looked stuck in the 90s but was clean and well cared for.

He walked in behind her. "Make yourself at home. Your room is down the hall, first door on the left."

"Okay. I'll be right back." She took her bag of personal items to the room and placed it on the double bed covered with a quaint blue and white quilt then found Peter in the kitchen. She dropped the other bag onto the counter. "My contribution to our provisions."

He peeked inside. "Hmm. Why am I not surprised by the hot chocolate?"

She shrugged. "It's comfort food, or rather, a comfort drink. Would you like a cup?"

"Maybe later. First, let's make dinner then put the pieces of this puzzle together. I feel like we're on the cusp of solving this case."

"I thought you weren't a detective," she challenged.

"Like you said, I know how to follow evidence." He unloaded the bags of groceries. "And I'm anxious to get this guy."

"Me too. I know the authorities are trying to find him, but it would be kind of fun to figure it out on our own."

"You enjoy mysteries?" He pulled a cutting board out of a cupboard then reached for a knife.

"I do, so long as I'm not the object of the mystery."

He chuckled. "I hear that. Will you rinse the lettuce while I get the onion chopped?"

"What are we having?"

"Chili, green salad, and sourdough bread."

"Sounds yummy."

"Chili is my kind of comfort food."

She got busy preparing the greens. She could get used to working side by side in the kitchen with Peter. The sizzle of the red onion sautéing in the skillet brought back fond memories of cooking with her mom when she was younger. She breathed in the warm scent.

Peter added ground beef to the skillet. Then, with a hand crank style can opener, he removed the tops of several varieties of beans. He poured them all into a pot, added spices, and stirred everything together.

"You're quite the cook," Jenna said.

"I have a few dishes I'm good at." He shot her a lopsided grin.

Her breath caught—Peter had to be the most attractive man she'd ever met, especially when he grinned. Good thing she suggested putting their relationship on hold until after the case was solved because being here alone with him would be too great of a temptation otherwise. One thing was certain—they had to figure this out before Monday.

23

The following morning, Jenna stood with hands on hips, studying the whiteboard Peter had pulled from the hall closet. Apparently, his aunt had been big on playing Pictionary.

Peter cleared his throat.

Jenna whirled toward the sound. "Good morning."

Peter's tousled hair, jeans, and T-shirt drew her like a butterfly to flowers. They *had* to solve this today. This case was the only thing stopping them from seeing where things would go between them. She was more determined than ever to figure it out. They'd stayed up late last night trying but had given up around midnight.

"Coffee." Peter padded into the kitchen and poured from the pot he'd programmed last night. He drank several gulps before easing onto a chair. "Do you always wake up so fresh and wide-eyed?"

She chuckled. "I'm a morning person."

"I'm not." He finished his coffee and placed the mug onto a coaster.

"I couldn't tell," she teased. "Are you hungry?"

He stood. "How do eggs and toast sound?"

"What, no donuts?" She shot a grin in his direction.

He pulled open a cupboard. "Actually…" He held up a box of prepackaged old-fashioned donuts.

Her eyes widened. "Those are my favorite." She strode to the kitchen and reached for the box.

He laughed. "Is that all you want?"

"Yep." She opened the box and pulled a donut from the top row. She bit into the tasty pastry and grinned. "You have no idea how much I love these. I didn't see them when you put them away."

"You were in your room."

She refilled her coffee mug then sat at the table while he scrambled a couple of eggs.

Peter plated his eggs, buttered his toast, then joined her at the table. He offered a blessing for their food then dug in.

Jenna waited for him to swallow before repeating her question. "Have you come up with any suspects?"

He grimaced. "Later. I need sustenance first. Gets my brain cells hopping."

She shook her head at the image. "You're kind of a nut."

"Thanks." He finished off his toast and washed it down with a second cup of coffee. "I hope you saved me a donut."

"As if I could eat all six." She rolled her eyes.

He stood, grabbed a donut from the box, and

motioned with his head toward the whiteboard. "I have three suspects."

A jolt of excitement shot through Jenna. "Who?"

"I'm working with the theory that your former boss, Josh, is in cahoots with someone at Kratt Paper."

"Really? I thought you believed him when he said he didn't know about the letters."

"We did, but other evidence has come to light. Did you know his sister is on the board there?"

"No. Wouldn't hiring Josh's ad company be a conflict of interest?"

"Some might argue that, but it's a private business, so that's up to them." He shrugged. "The most interesting thing I've discovered is that Samantha and Josh's sister were college friends."

"Seriously?" Jenna didn't know her former boss had a sister. "How old is she? She must be older, considering her position at Kratt Paper."

"Trina is thirty-two." His gaze met hers. "I think his sister is behind the notes."

"What about the bomb?"

He rubbed the back of his neck. "I haven't figured that out yet. According to my source, Trina was out of town the night of the bombing."

"What about Josh?" Jenna had a hard time believing her former boss could be a bomber, but she had to ask.

"He was at home. Alone."

"No one can vouch for him?" Jenna asked. "What about security cameras or a neighbor that might have seen him?"

Peter grinned. "You're pretty good at this. Frank told the lead police detective our suspicions."

"And?" Why did this man insist on stringing her along?

"No one noticed him coming or going."

Jenna's shoulders slumped. "So he was inside all night." She'd really wanted him to be the bomber since he'd almost ruined her life. Okay, that might be a slight exaggeration. "Where does Samantha fit into all of this?"

"My theory is she wanted your job and was willing to do anything to get it."

Jenna gasped. "Do you think she's the one who posted the video?"

Peter winced. He stood and took his dishes to the sink. "I did something you asked me not to." He hadn't planned to tell her, but if he wanted things to progress between him and Jenna, keeping secrets needed to stop. "I followed up with a cyber expert. It took some footwork on my part, but I was able to track the video upload to a phone registered to Ads by Design. After even more investigating, it appears the phone is assigned to Samantha."

Jenna blinked rapidly, and her face paled.

Good thing she still sat at the kitchen table. He filled a glass with water. "Drink this. It will help ease the shock."

"Doubtful." She drank the water anyway. "I can't believe I thought we were friends. But if Trina and Samantha are friends, why would she post that video of me slamming their company?"

"She benefited from your departure."

"True, but the question remains the same."

He shrugged. "I'm guessing she figured she could get away with it. We won't know until we ask her."

Jenna laughed drily. "Right. The last time we spoke she was less than friendly. I don't think she'd willingly tell us anything."

"She doesn't have to."

Jenna tipped her head to the side. "What aren't you telling me? And since you have all this figured out, who was following us?"

"No idea. The plates were stolen."

Jenna groaned. "Figures. I hate this. What *do* we know?"

He dipped his chin. "Nothing. This is all conjecture."

She rolled her eyes. "Conjecture or not, it makes sense. Are the authorities aware of your theories?"

"The ideas came to me as I was going to sleep last night. I called Frank and explained everything. We'd already tossed out a couple of these ideas as not being plausible, so I'm not sure he bought what I had to say."

"Well, that's stupid."

He chuckled. "I appreciate that, but Frank is a good guy. He'll do due diligence." She was cute when she was perturbed—kissable. He tripped over the thought and shook his head.

"What?" Jenna's brown eyes held curiosity.

"Just a thought I need to ignore."

"Seems to me stream of consciousness might be a good way to figure this out."

"Trust me that thought wasn't helpful."

Her face pinked. Could she read his mind?

He needed to put some space between them before he did something he shouldn't. They weren't far from a park with a beach. He'd spent many childhood days watching for whales from the shoreline. "What do you say we go down to the water? Maybe we'll spot a whale."

"I guess. It's better than sitting around here all day." She stood. "Let me grab my jacket."

"It's on the hook beside the door." He'd hung it there last night after she'd left it on a chair.

"Oh. I'll brush my teeth then be right back."

As he walked to the master bath to do the same, he shot off a text to Frank for an update. His screen lit up.

Hang tight. The police have a lead. This thing looks bigger than we imagined. Lay low. I'll be in touch.

Indecision warred in him. He'd already suggested whale watching. If he changed plans now, Jenna might suspect something was up. Was that so bad? He shook his head. She didn't need to know until he had something more to report. He quickly brushed his teeth then covered his head with a beanie cap.

Jenna stood by the door. She'd donned her coat. "Nice hat."

"Thanks." He slipped into his jacket and palmed his keys that were in the pocket. "You ready?"

She nodded.

He pulled open the door and a gust of wind blasted in. "You sure you want to go out right now?"

"Not if it's going to be this windy."

"There must be a storm blowing in. Most times when I'm here, there are relatively calm winds."

She slipped out of her coat. "Now what do we do?"

"There are plenty of games and puzzles."

She shook her head. "I don't have patience for either. What about books?"

He grinned. "As a matter of fact, my aunt was an avid reader of Christian fiction. Follow me." He went to the last door in the hall and pushed it open. A floor to ceiling built-in bookshelf covered one wall. The cozy window nook had scattered pillows. A recliner rested in the corner, and a round table sat in the middle of the room. "Aunt Charlotte hosted a book club once a week."

"Wow. That's often."

"She loved books, and she loved talking about them. The characters in those stories were her companions. They were as real to her as you or I."

"Double wow." She scrunched her face. "Was she mentally stable?"

He laughed. "Yes. There was nothing wrong with

my aunt's mental acuity. She was quite intelligent and simply loved fiction. Do you enjoy reading?"

"Yes." Jenna moved toward the huge bookshelf and rolling ladder. She stepped onto the ladder then looked at him over her shoulder. "I've always wanted one of these ladders."

He chuckled. "You look like a child in a toy store."

"I feel like one too. Don't you want to pick one?"

He shook his head. "I prefer non-fiction."

She shrugged. "Your loss." Ten minutes later, she curled up on the window seat book in hand.

He prayed that would keep her worries at bay. Jenna had more than enough to stress her out, and another day to simply relax would be good for her. Meanwhile, he had a hunch to follow up on.

24

Thunder punctuated the air. "One one-thousand." Dad had taught her to count after a rumble to see how far away the lightning was. "Two one-thousand." Lightning flashed. Jenna shivered and closed the book. She wasn't afraid of storms generally speaking, but this one appeared worse than average. Wind whipped the branches of the seventy-plus-foot fir trees around the property. Would the wind be strong enough to blow one over? Were they safe?

The window rattled, propelling her off the seat and out the library door in search of Peter. She found him in the living room watching football. "The lightning is only two miles away." She curled up on the opposite end of the couch. "Did your aunt ever have a tree fall in a storm?"

"Not that I recall. Are you worried?" He glanced her way for a moment before returning his attention to the game.

"A little. The wind is really moving those branches.

Plus with the rain we've had lately, the ground is already soft."

"The trees here are healthy. I don't think we need to worry about one falling onto the house, but to be safe, we should stay away from the windows in case any branches break off and go flying in the wind."

She sucked in a breath. "I hadn't thought of that. I'm sure glad we're inside and didn't get caught out in this."

"Me too." The TV flickered. He reached for the remote and clicked it off. "It's not a good game anyway."

"If this storm takes its merry time, you might need to give Brandi a call and let her know you'll be late tomorrow."

"Okay. I'll give my parents a call too since it looks like we won't make dinner tonight. Are you sure we'll need to spend an extra night here?" They had planned to head back to Seattle later today. She didn't blame him for not wanting to drive with the treacherous rain and wind.

"It's possible we could head back after the storm, but I don't want to take you back to Seattle with someone on the loose intending you harm."

"I can't stay in hiding, Peter. I have a life—at least I'm trying to. Besides, they haven't done anything to harm me." *Yet.* Was she even safe here? Somehow the letter writer had known about her new apartment when she hadn't told anyone except her dad and Peter. Her eyes widened. "What if I have a stalker?"

He seemed unfazed by the pronouncement. "It's possible. And he's very good at remaining concealed."

She frowned. "How would you know that unless…?" Her gaze smacked into his.

"I was following you?"

She nodded.

"It was my job to keep an eye on you. You already knew that." He shrugged. "Sally relieved me from time to time."

"I feel so stupid. How could I not have known I was being followed?" Her stomach knotted. She'd always considered herself to be alert and aware of her surroundings. Apparently, that wasn't true if Peter had managed to avoid her detection.

He reached for her hand. "I'm good at what I do. Don't beat yourself up." He gave her hand a gentle squeeze before releasing it and standing. "How about some hot chocolate. That's sure to make you feel better."

"No, thanks." Her stomach was a mess.

His brow furrowed. "Stop worrying."

She stood and paced to the window. "I can't help it. I have a foreboding I can't shake."

Peter's hands rested on her shoulders as she looked out the window. Tingles shot through her at his touch.

"No one knows where we are. You're safe here," Peter said softly.

"How can you be so certain? I mean, you were able to follow me for days undetected. How do you know someone didn't follow us?"

"I'm a professional, trained to spot a tail."

She blew out a breath, releasing pent up stress. He was right. Other than the storm, there was nothing to be afraid of.

A knock sounded on the door.

Jenna jumped. Her eyes widened as she whirled to face Peter. "Someone's here," she whispered.

"Go barricade yourself in one of the bedrooms. It's probably one of the neighbors coming to check on the house."

"They do that?" Doubt filled her as her heart rate accelerated.

"Just go, Jenna. Please, hurry." He turned and strode toward the front door.

Jenna darted to her room and pushed the chest of drawers in front of the door. Breathing hard, she sat on the floor in front of it and closed her eyes. *Lord, we need You. Please protect us.*

Jenna opened her eyes at the sound of a familiar voice. *Polly?* She stood and pushed the dresser aside just enough to open the door. She strained to hear the voices.

"A tree's blocking the road. I was hoping you'd be able to help."

That sure sounded like her old assistant, but what was she doing all the way up here in Warm Beach? Her pulse thrummed in her ears. Could Polly be behind her trouble? As quickly as the thought came, Jenna dismissed it. Polly didn't have it in her to be so cruel.

Her assistant was sweet and loyal. That had to be someone else talking to Peter.

"There's a chainsaw in the shed. Let me get my raincoat, and I'll see what I can do."

"Thank you. That's so nice of you."

Jenna eased the door open further then crept along the hall. She peeked around the corner and gasped. It was Polly! Her heart pounded. Had she misread Polly the same way she'd misread Samantha?

There was one way to find out if Polly was behind all the trouble. "Peter," she called out before walking into the entryway. She feigned surprise. "Polly? What are you doing here?" Her former assistant was only an inch or two shorter than Peter's five-foot-eleven inches.

Polly's eyes widened. "Jenna. I sure didn't expect to see you way out here. How have you been?"

Jenna shrugged. "Since leaving Ads by Design it's been a challenge. I heard you were let go. I'm really sorry that happened to you too."

"Thanks." Polly looked at Peter. "Jenna seems to have the hand of God on her life. No matter what happens, she manages to bounce back. She even managed to land a man like you." She shook her head and reached for the doorknob. "Shall we?"

Peter shot her a look that asked, "What's-her-story?"

Jenna shook her head then froze when Polly looked directly at her. "It was great to see you again, Jenna." She walked out.

A cold chill ran through Jenna.

Peter closed and locked the door then turned to face Jenna. "Stay here and lock up after me. I have keys. Don't open it for anyone. Got it?"

She nodded. "Polly was my assistant and loyal to a fault. She would never try to hurt me. At least, I don't think she would."

"People can surprise you." He stepped toward her, took her hand, and gave it a quick squeeze. "Whatever happens, look out for you, and don't worry about me." He drew her to him and kissed her. "I don't know what I'd do if anything happened to you. There's a small revolver in the nightstand in my room. My aunt kept it for protection since she lived alone. Do you know how to use one?"

Jenna nodded, though it'd been years since her dad had taken her to the shooting range.

"Good. Lock the door." He yanked it open.

A gust of wind blew in, lifting her hair from her shoulders. She quickly locked up and went to find the revolver.

Polly had always had her back. She was the one person from Ads by Design she knew she could rely on and trust, but yet she couldn't shake a niggling of doubt.

Peter pulled the chainsaw from the shed then walked beside Polly along the driveway, keeping a little distance between them. He didn't trust this woman, regardless of what Jenna said.

"How long have you and Jenna been dating? It must be a new thing since she never mentioned it at work."

"We aren't dating." Large raindrops pelted him and created puddles on the ground.

"Oh. I assumed since the two of you were here together. Never mind."

The rain increased, making him wish he was still indoors. "So you were Jenna's assistant. How was she to work for?" he shouted above the roar of the increasing wind and rain.

"Fine."

He glanced toward her. "That's it? Seems to me she's a force to be reckoned with. I imagine she could be demanding." Stranger things had happened, but he couldn't shake that something was off with Polly. When they'd done a background check on her, no red flags had been raised, but the fact that she was here now sent more than a little suspicion in her direction.

"Demanding, yes. But working with Jenna was great training. After all, I was only supposed to be a summer intern. I should be grateful I lasted an extra month."

Should be? "You're not grateful?" Ahead a red Ford Focus was stopped in the middle of the road right in front of his driveway. He looked more closely and sure enough, a small tree blocked the roadway. Maybe Polly being here was as innocent as she claimed, but her arrival and the color of her car were still too much of a coincidence. His gut said she was up to no good.

"I am grateful. I didn't mean to insinuate I wasn't. She taught me a lot about the ad business."

"That's great. At least your time there wasn't a waste." The tree looked slight enough to pull off to the side of the road—even Polly could have done it if she tried. He set the chainsaw down on his driveway, changed his mind, then reached for it again. Something slammed into his head. Had a branch hit him? He closed his eyes trying to think through the intense pain shooting through his cranium. "What was that?" Bleary-eyed, he looked at Polly who stood above him holding a gun. His pulse amped. "Whoa." He started to raise his hands.

Polly whipped her arm up and came down hard on his head with the butt of the gun.

He dropped to his knees. Everything went black.

Pounding on the front door drew Jenna from the bedroom. Peter and Polly had only been gone a short while. Were they back already?

Jenna looked through the peephole and spotted Polly. Alone. She slipped the gun into the back of the waistline of her jeans like she'd seen people do on TV. What should she do? Peter said not to open the door for anyone.

"Jenna open up. Peter's hurt." Polly pounded on the door again.

Jenna's heart kicked into double time. Peter was hurt. She had to help him. He would do the same for her if the situation was reversed. She flipped the lock and yanked open the door. "What happened?"

"A tree limb broke, hitting him and knocking him out."

Jenna looked past Polly. "You left him out there?"

"He's too big for me to carry. I figured the two of us could get him back here together."

"Okay." Jenna reached for her jacket on the hook beside the door.

Her former assistant stepped past her. "Close the door, Jenna."

With her side to Polly she slipped on the jacket. "I have to go help him. We can't abandon him to the elements. It's horrible out there."

"It's about to be more horrible in here." Polly's voice held a sinister tone.

Jenna stilled then turned to face the younger woman who held a revolver pointed at her. "You're my stalker?" Her stomach dropped.

"Why so surprised?" Polly waved the gun. "You cost me my job. Do you have any idea how hard it is to find work when you were the personal assistant to the most hated woman of the moment?"

"Polly, please put down the gun."

"My name is Pauline!" Polly sucked in a sharp breath. "I hate that stupid nickname."

Jenna backed against the front door. "I'm sorry, I didn't know. Is that what this is about? Me calling you Polly?"

Pauline rolled her eyes. "Please. This is about so much more. It's about being invisible. You see me now, don't you?" She aimed the revolver at Jenna's chest.

Jenna pressed harder against the door. "You have never been invisible to me. I told everyone what a great assistant you were, and I even sent a text to check on you when I learned you'd been let go."

Confusion filled Polly…Pauline's face. "I didn't get any messages from you."

Jenna thought back to the night Samantha had told her about Polly then sighed. "But I sent you one. I can show you on my phone."

Polly narrowed her eyes. "Don't move."

"But I can show you the message."

"Too late." She waved the gun in the air. "After all the mistakes you've made, you deserve what's coming to you." She cocked the gun.

"Wait, if you're going to kill me at least fill in the blanks. What mistakes are you talking about?"

Polly sneered. "It's pathetic that you don't know."

Jenna had to find a way to keep Polly talking until help arrived. Panic surged through her. What if no one came to rescue her? What if the only person on the planet who knew her location was dead? "At least tell me what happened to Peter? Did a branch really hit him?"

"I cold-cocked him."

Jenna gasped.

"You have always underestimated me. I graduated the top of my class with a double major in chemical engineering and advertising."

"That's an odd combination." She sucked in a sharp breath—the pipe bombs. Anyone could easily find out how to make one, but it would be child's play for a chemical engineer. But why had Polly done it?

"Stop judging me! You aren't my mentor anymore. Did you know I wanted to work with you? I actually requested to be your assistant. I admired your work and wanted to learn from the best."

Jenna shook her head, too afraid to voice her response.

"But you had no time for me. You never let me do anything more exciting than prepare the budget for your potential projects."

"That's not entirely true. What I had you doing was the foundation of advertising. Your budget determines what you can do. I taught you other things as well. By the time your internship was over, you knew everything about how to do my job."

"Sure. Because you had me do everything except what I wanted to do."

"Which was?"

"Create."

Movement caught Jenna's eye, but she fought to keep her focus on Polly.

"Seems to me your creativity is what got you into this mess," Jenna said.

Peter slipped silently into the room behind Polly with his gun trained on her.

"Did you record me and uploaded the video to the Internet?"

Polly smirked.

"But why? By doing that, your job was right in the middle of the falling dominoes of my life. You sabotaged yourself." She fought to keep from looking to the still-silent Peter for an explanation. "If you hadn't uploaded that video then neither of us would have been let go."

Polly closed her eyes, wincing. "Shut up. This is your fault. You were the princess at Ads by Design. Everyone thought you could do no wrong. Josh loved you by the way. Oh, he was professional enough to hide his feelings, but I could tell. Men are such fools. Why couldn't he see you only care about yourself?"

Clearly, Polly was delusional. Josh had zero feelings for Jenna, or he wouldn't have let her go or ignored the threats to her life. Jenna swallowed the lump in her throat and lowered her voice. "I'm so sorry you feel that way, Polly. I do care about people, but I suppose my tenacity at work made it look otherwise."

"You were the best. You didn't have to walk over others to prove it."

"I didn't realize I did. I don't know what else to say. Other than to apologize." Had she really been so awful?

Sure, she'd been focused on the job and didn't socialize with her co-workers. But she wasn't ruthless like Polly accused. Maybe she'd been a little self-absorbed, but she'd changed.

Peter moved within a foot of Polly. How did the woman not sense him right behind her?

"Why'd you do it?" Peter asked.

Polly startled and whirled around. She fired her gun wildly.

Peter knocked her gun to the floor, holstered his, then twisted Polly's arms behind her back. He pulled zip-tie cuffs from his back pocket and had her secured in under a minute.

Polly sank to the floor. "I hate you," she cried.

Peter rushed to Jenna's side. "Are you okay?"

"Yes." She reached up but stopped herself from touching the goose egg on the back of his head. "What about you?"

"I'll live. I've already called 9-1-1. Help is on the way."

25

Jenna sat between Sally and Peter in Frank's office. Marc and Carissa, sat off to the side. "What's going to happen to Polly?"

"It's too soon to say for sure," Frank said. "She's scheduled for a mental health evaluation, and she's facing a lot of charges. I expect she'll spend many years behind bars."

Jenna laced her fingers together. "Of all the people in that office, I thought she would be the one I could trust the most."

"Her jealousy of you festered," Sally said. "She wanted what you had and saw her opportunity to grab it when you lost your temper. She expected to step into your shoes."

"Did she send the first e-mail?"

"No. One of the men in the office sent it as a joke." Frank handed her an envelope.

"What's this?"

"An apology. Apparently, your former co-worker

heard about what went down with Pauline and decided to come clean."

Jenna tucked the envelope into her purse. Her mind already in overload, she'd deal with the apology later. "There's one thing I still don't understand. Why did Polly deliver the notes to the office for a week?"

"We aren't sure she did. Josh swore he knew nothing about them." Frank's eyes widened, and he motioned toward the bullpen. "Looks like we have company."

Sally stood. "I'll deal with her."

Jenna looked over her shoulder and surprise shot through her. "Why is Samantha here?"

"Good question," Frank said. "Bring her in, Sally."

A moment later a pale-faced Samantha walked in ahead of Sally. "Umm, hi."

Frank motioned to Sally's empty chair. "Please sit."

Samantha eased onto the seat. "I'm sorry for not making an appointment. I heard about what Polly did, and I wanted to clear something up."

Jenna's heart pounded. She wasn't sure she could handle one more surprise, but it appeared she had little choice in the matter.

"I recorded the video of your rant on my phone, but I didn't upload it. Please believe me."

"Are you suggesting Pauline did that?" Frank asked. "We were under the impression that Pauline recorded the video too."

Samantha shook her head. "I'm ashamed to admit it

was me. She knew the password to my phone, and I keep it in my desk at work. Based on everything I've heard, I'm sure she uploaded it."

That explained so much, including why Polly never admitted to recording her rant.

I'm so sorry," Samantha went on. "There's more." She ducked her chin. "The notes that I gave you were actually slid under my apartment door."

"Why'd you lie?" Jenna asked.

"I was scared. I went to Josh for help. I thought if I told him I'd found them at the office he'd help us. Instead, he wanted nothing to do with them and made me promise to destroy them and not tell anyone. He was afraid more bad publicity would ruin his company."

She shouldn't be surprised that Josh was such a good liar. He was able to fool two seasoned cops. She had sure read her former boss wrong. "You could have told me the truth, Samantha. Speaking of which, why didn't you give me the notes since they had my name on them?"

"I had planned to." She shrugged. "I was curious, and they weren't sealed. Then I saw what was inside...I wanted to protect you. I figured it was one of your haters."

"Who knew where I was staying?" Jenna thought Samantha was smarter than that. She directed her attention to Frank. "How did Polly know where I was all this time? I assumed she was stalking me, but Peter said no one followed us to Warm Beach."

"And he was correct. Pauline had an app on her phone that allowed her to track your phone."

Jenna blew out a long, slow breath. She had asked Polly to set up the app after misplacing her phone for a day, but she never dreamed the woman would use it to stalk her.

Peter reached for her hand. "Are you okay?"

"Yeah. It's all a bit overwhelming though."

Frank tapped his desk with a pen. "There's one more thing. Pauline was able to escape detection when she left the notes at your apartment because she has a friend who lives a couple doors away from yours."

"Wow. Talk about dumb luck. What about your musician client? He was threatened too."

"Based on the statement Pauline gave to the police, she was concerned the letters she'd sent you could be tracked to her, so to throw the authorities off her trail she went after the man who publicly supported you."

"That explains why the first letters were mailed to him," Peter said, "rather than hand-delivered. But the pipe bombs were a bit much. If this was all motivated by losing her job, why risk hurting innocent people?"

Frank shrugged. "And that is the million-dollar question. Which is one reason why she's being given a mental health exam."

Samantha cleared her throat. "If I may?" She looked at Frank.

"By all means. Fill in the blanks."

"I knew Pauline from college. When she was a

freshman, I was her senior mentor. She was fascinated with explosive devices. I was concerned and encouraged her to check out an advertising degree instead. She liked the idea and pursued it. After I graduated, we kept in touch, which is why she applied for the mentorship at Ads by Design."

"What's that have to do with the bomb?" Frank asked.

"I suppose it's not exactly related except she likes to blow up things."

Peter sighed. "Maybe we'll never know her motivation. But I think it's safe to assume, she's an angry, and likely, a mentally unstable person."

Jenna nodded. "It might be too little too late, but I've learned a lesson in all of this."

"What's that?" Sally asked.

"Everyone is significant and needs to feel like others see them. And I must work at always being kind and cut people some slack because I have no idea what they're dealing with."

"Reminds me of my credo," Sally said.

"What's that?" Jenna asked.

"Ephesians 4:32, 'Be kind and compassionate to one another, forgiving each other, just as in Christ God forgave you.'"

Samantha huffed a breath. "Easier said than done."

"That's for sure." Jenna shifted to face Samantha. "I probably owe you an apology based on what Polly said."

"Pauline." Every voice in the room chimed in at once.

Jenna's faced heated. "Pauline. Anyway, if I ever did anything to make you feel trampled over or insignificant, I'm sorry. It wasn't intentional, but that's no excuse."

"Apology accepted."

Marc shifted in his seat. "We've covered Jenna and Tom, but what about Jason?"

Frank frowned. "All we know is the perpetrator was out for justice. He blamed Jason for the paper company polluting the Sound. The police didn't indicate Pauline had anything to do with that. From what I understand Jenna's viral video set off the perpetrator."

Jenna blew out a breath. "I'm so glad this is finally over. I can't thank all of you enough." She could finally move on with her life.

With his arm across Jenna's shoulders, Peter strolled along the wharf. So far, their first date had been everything he'd hoped for. "Would you like to ride the Great Wheel?"

She wrapped her arm across her stomach. "I'm too stuffed. Thanks for dinner."

He chuckled. "You already thanked me." She'd devoured the fish and chips they each ordered at her favorite seafood place on the wharf.

"I know, but it was such a treat."

"I'm glad. Are you sure you don't want to ride the Great Wheel?" he pressed.

"No, thanks. I'm not a fan of Ferris wheels. I like to keep my feet firmly planted on the ground. No more going in circles for me."

"That's a good place for them." He gave her shoulders a light squeeze. He wanted this night to last forever, but they both had to work in the morning. Frank had another assignment for him—protecting a local celebrity. He didn't mind the job, but what Frank was working on seemed far more fascinating. Kratt Paper had caught his boss's attention, and he wasn't letting it go. It would be interesting to see what Frank discovered. Peter only hoped he didn't get hurt in the process.

Jenna stopped and looked up at him. "We should do this again soon."

He pulled her with him out of the path of walkers. "I'd like that. What do you say next time we go whale watching?"

"Sounds like fun as long as I can stay firmly on solid ground."

"You get seasick?" He winced. At least there were plenty of beaches to watch the whales from along the Puget Sound.

She nodded. "It'll be fun. I'll make us a picnic."

"It's a bit cold for a picnic."

"When you live in the Pacific Northwest you adapt." She playfully poked his chest.

He wrapped his hands around hers. "I can adapt." He tucked a strand of hair behind her ears. Her eyes met his as he lowered his mouth to hers, savoring the taste of her soft lips.

Jenna leaned away.

"What?"

"Just enjoying the moment."

He tugged her closer. "You're not doing it right." He captured her lips again, deepening the kiss.

Jenna sighed. "I could get used to this," she murmured.

"Me too." His heart soared in anticipation of their future.

Epilogue

Marc sat outside on Carissa's balcony on a lounge chair facing her. He zipped his coat to help ward off the chill in the damp air. A book rested on his lap—not his preferred way to spend his day off, but any off-time with Carissa was worth the sacrifice.

"Stop staring." Carissa kept her eyes focused on her book.

"I'm not."

She glanced up and met his gaze. "You sure about that?" Her eyes danced with mirth. She'd been more light-hearted since visiting a counselor.

"Well…I could use a different book. What else do you have?"

"There's a graphic novel on the shelf inside."

He looked at the thriller in his hands, which was actually a great book. He simply wasn't in the mood to sit still. "Want to take a walk?"

"And risk running into trouble?" She shook her head. "No, thank you. I can't seem to leave home without getting sucked into work." She rearranged the blanket she had wrapped over herself. Though technically still too cold and wet to be enjoying the outdoors, her covered balcony had enough protection for the hardy.

"Can we talk?" he asked.

She set her book aside and pulled her knees to her chest. "About what?"

"I don't know." He scrambled for a topic. "Do you remember last summer when we talked about how God cares about the little things?"

She nodded.

"I've been chewing on that idea since then as well, and I've noticed something."

"What's that?" She asked.

"In our business we see a lot of rotten stuff and run into the worst kind of people, yet at the same time, I'm hopeful because I know that God is in control. Even when it seems like all hope is lost. I've come to realize that the small stuff matters to Him." He chuckled. "He even put Jenna and Peter together."

"Are you suggesting God is a matchmaker?" A twinkle lit Carissa's eyes.

"Why not? He's in the details. Right down to putting you in the right place to help Hannah. You love coffee, and it's because of that love that you built a friendship with her. It's because of that relationship that she felt comfortable coming to you when she needed help. Honestly, I don't think she would have talked to anyone else, and who knows where she'd be right now if she hadn't."

Carissa quirked a grin. "So you're saying that God used my love of coffee to not only help Hannah but knew it would give me joy to be surrounded by the rich scent of coffee for four hours a day?"

He nodded. "It's as if He takes delight in delighting us."

"I never thought about that before, but I think you're right." Her brows furrowed. "How do you explain that you not only hate coffee, but you don't care for the smell either, and you were stuck there too?"

He shrugged. "I was more than happy to tolerate the circumstances to work alongside you." His heart tripped. He had almost said, "I love you." Were they ready to go there?

"Has anyone ever told you you're sweet?"

He shrugged again, his face warming. He stood and headed inside. "Think I'll go grab a soda." *Coward.* Sure, he was backpedaling, but he didn't want to risk losing Carissa because he lacked patience. When the time was right, he'd tell her how deep his feelings for her went. He pulled open the refrigerator door and reached for a can of soda.

Footsteps sounded on the wood flooring. "Did you want something from the fridge," he said without looking over his shoulder.

Carissa's arms slid around his waist. Her head rested against his back. "I'm good."

He closed the door and slowly turned to face her. "I could get used to this."

"Good." She looked up at him. Her hands slid to his chest and moved up until they wrapped around his neck.

He lowered his head and captured her lips. Tingles zipped through him as he deepened the kiss.

Carissa groaned and tilted her head back. "We should stop."

He dropped his arms to his side, immediately missing the feel of her beneath his hands. "Ready for that walk now?" He winked.

She chuckled. "You win."

He'd won for sure. He'd won the heart of a strong woman with a passion to help others. It didn't get better to his way of thinking. He draped an arm across her shoulders. "Where to?"

"Anywhere, so long as it's with you."

Author Note

I hope you enjoyed reading *Imminent Threat*. It was a unique experience writing it because I blended two shorter stories together to create one larger work. The next book in this series will release in the fall. It will feature Frank and take place the week of Christmas. Often times I'm asked who my favorite character is in a book and I'm willing to admit that Frank is my favorite character in this series. I'm so excited to write his story.

If you enjoyed this book, I hope you will take the time to write a short review on Amazon or any other book site you use. Thanks in advance!

If you want to learn more about me or my books please check out my website kimberlyrjohnson.com

If you've read my Bride's of Seattle series you might be wondering if the Brandi and Katie in this book are the same women featured in that series. The answer is yes. For those curious about Brandi and Ian's romance you'll want to check out *Until I Met You*, the prequel to the Bride's of Seattle series. If you want to know Katie's story, you'll find that in *The Reluctant Groom*. Please note that series is a contemporary romance series and not mystery or suspense like the book you just finished reading.

In conclusion the publication of a book took a small village. I want to extend special thanks to my critique group, editor, proofreaders, beta readers and early readers. All of you have helped make this book what it is. I appreciate each and every one of you!

I also want to extend special thanks to those of you who held me up in prayer. Getting this series ready to publish during a pandemic has been an emotional challenge. One would think it would be easier, but for this very introverted woman who loves to write in complete silence, having my family home—one attending university online and another working from home has presented unexpected challenges. But with prayer and determination the first two books will release on time, and the third book will be ready by fall.

Blessings,
Kimberly Rose Johnson

More Books by
Kimberly Rose Johnson

Protection Inc.
Direct Threat

Law Enforcement Heroes
Edge of Truth

The Librarian Sleuth
The Sleuth's Miscalculation
The Sleuth's Dilemma
The Sleuth's Conundrum
The Sleuth's Surprise (September 2020)

Brides of Seattle
Until I Met You
The Reluctant Groom
Simply Smitten

Melodies of Love
A Love Song for Kayla
An Encore for Estelle
A Waltz for Amber

Sunriver Dreams
A Love to Treasure
A Christmas Homecoming
Designing Love

Wildflower B&B Romance Series
Island Refuge
Island Dreams
Island Christmas
Island Hope

Contemporary Novellas
Brewed with Love
Sara's Gift